CRAIG HALLORAN

Contact Information

Dragon Wars: Claws and Steel - Book 12

By Craig Halloran

★ ★ ★ ★ ★

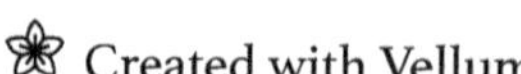 Created with Vellum

Gapoli
Ice Vale
Dark Mountain
Ugrad
Far Stick
Loose Boot
Black Stow
Crack Scowl
Green Ridge
Agustun
Staatus
Kenna
Dagger Ford
Doverun
The Great River
Inland Sea
Arrow Wood
Westerlund
Monarch City
Naalum
Ferry Lunn
Portam
Harbor Lake
Raven Cliff
The Outer Ring
Part of the Willowacks
Mortus
Iron Hills
Red Bone
Salt Knob
Oldham
Havenstock
Farhook
Valley Shire
Sulter Slay
Pebble Bolt
Hotvale
Lake Flugge
Gunder Island
Gold Hook
Littleton
Crow Valley
Dwarf Skull
The Shelf

THE SHELF

"HOW ARE YOU FEELING BACK THERE?" Streak hollered.

Grey Cloak had a tight grip on Streak's reins, and his feet were stuffed into the stirrups of the dragon's saddle. His stomach tossed from side to side, and he could barely speak. "Could you slow down?"

"Who wants to go slowly when you can go fast?" Streak beat his wings and jetted across the bright sky like he'd been shot from a bow. "How's that?"

"Awful," Grey Cloak groaned. He hunkered over the saddle with his jaw clenched. For the last few days, he and Dyphestive had begun training as dragon riders, but no matter what Grey Cloak tried, his stomach wound up in knots.

"Is your tummy still bothering you?" Streak asked as he turned his head around and winked. "Let's try this."

Grey Cloak knew what Streak was going to do before he did it. "No, not that!"

The middling twin-tailed dragon did a loop the loop a thousand feet above the ground. He followed it up with twin barrel rolls and a twist that ended in another loop.

"Enough, Streak! Enough! Take me down!"

"I hear you," Streak said in a sad voice. His wings flattened out, and he glided in a slow circle toward the ground. "But you're bound to get used to it. You need to keep flying."

Grey Cloak shook his head. *How can I be a Sky Rider that gets sick in the sky?* The thought of it sickened him.

"Hey, Grey, what's going on? Are you sick again?" Dyphestive hollered from somewhere nearby.

Grey Cloak turned his head to the left. Dyphestive was riding on Rock, a monster of a grand dragon, with a flat head like Streak's, great horns, and all dark scales.

Dyphestive sat upright in the saddle with the wind rustling his hair, as proud as a peacock. He had a big smile on his face and let out a gusty laugh. "This is great, isn't it?"

"If Streak would fly in a straight line, it might be." Grey Cloak kicked his dragon with his heel. "But he won't listen to me!"

"Hey, now. I listen, but it's hard to hear with the wind whistling by my earholes," Streak replied with a snicker.

Feather, a middling dragon with pink eyes and splashes

of pink scales, dropped from above and flew alongside Streak. "Is he sick again?"

Streak nodded.

"Ah, poor thing," Feather said with a sympathetic look.

Fenora joined the growing flock in the sky and sailed close to Streak. She was a grand dragon with jade eyes and a lot of attitude. "So, the little person is sick? Not sure why we need a little person. We can handle this war without riders."

"Agreed!" Rock responded in his deep voice.

Anya dropped in from the southern horizon. She rode on Cinder, with her waves of sun-bleached auburn hair flowing behind her. In her commanding voice, she said, "Is there a reason we have stopped running sky drills?"

"The little person is sick again," Fenora replied.

Grey Cloak looked at Anya and saw the disappointment in her face. He shrugged.

"Did you take your ginger root?" Anya shouted.

"I did," he said. It was a lie. The ginger root tasted awful, and he had no desire to eat it. "Did you take yours?"

Anya gave him a haughty look. "I don't need it. Everyone, listen to me. We are going to finish these drills. Sick or not! What are you going to do in battle, Grey Cloak, if your belly hurts? Surrender?"

Grey Cloak narrowed his eyes on her.

"Everyone, follow my lead! We'll form a wedge and go

into attack formation." She glanced at Dyphestive. "Ready your javelins!"

Dyphestive filled his big mitt with a javelin from Rock's oversize quivers. "Ready!" He gave Grey Cloak a sympathetic look and nodded.

"Are we still going down, brother?" Streak asked.

"No." Grey Cloak shook his head, loosened his feet from the stirrups, let go of the reins, and said, "You go on. I've had my fill of Anya. I'm bailing out." He jumped from the saddle, did a flip in the air, and plunged toward the ground, leaving everyone gasping.

2

HEAD DOWNWARD, Grey Cloak torpedoed toward the rocky, hard-packed terrain of the Shelf. With the hot winds ripping at his cloak, the ground closed in, and he twisted, turning his plunging body upright with less than one hundred feet between him and the barren plains.

The Cloak of Legends blossomed fifty feet from the earth. Grey Cloak floated slowly toward the gritty sands with his arms crossed and a smirk on his face. He touched down softly near Nath, and the cloak collapsed around his body.

"A nice trick," Nath said in his raspy voice. His long gray hair was shaggy, but the sun revealed rich streaks of bright red in his locks. The old man's build was as solid as stone, and he still stood taller, even with a hunch in his back. "You even had me fooled for a moment. And I think Feather left some dragon droppings over there."

Grey Cloak patted Nath's shoulder. "If you could only have seen the look on Anya's face when I dropped." He laughed. "That was priceless."

Nath scratched the scraggly hairs in his beard and said, "The pair of you are fire and water."

"I take it I'm the water?"

"Oh, without a doubt. Anya keeps her fire burning. That is her motivation. She has to stay angry to stay focused."

Grey Cloak watched the dragon riders blazing through the sky and said, "Being mad all the time is no way to live."

Nath gave him a hard-eyed look and, with a deadly serious tone, said, "This isn't about living. This is about survival."

"You don't have to tell me that. I know as well as anyone, and I've seen my friends die too. Anya isn't the only one with loss." He crossed his arms and kicked a stone away. "She is blinded by vengeance, but in my heart, I know a better way. It wasn't so long ago that we agreed to go to the Wizard Watch, and now she backpedals and says we need to train. I thought she wanted to get this over with."

"No one wins a war in a day. Believe me. I've fought in many." Nath shrugged his hunched shoulders. "And I admit I am fond of your plan, but you can't do that alone either. You'll need to work together."

Grey Cloak took a seat on a small boulder and said, "Is that how you won the wars that you fought? As a team?"

Nath offered an easy smile and sat on the same boulder beside Grey Cloak. "I thought I could do it alone. Believe me. I thought so more than anyone. But my team helped save me from myself, as well as many others." His golden-brown eyes watered. "I miss them. It's hard, even for me, knowing that you might not ever see someone again. Sometimes they never come back, and you realize that there were so many things you wished you could have said to them."

"Speaking of friends, I miss many of mine now. We need to find Zora and the others. We shouldn't have left them behind."

"They will find their way back to you. Good friends always do."

Grey Cloak nodded. "Then your friends should find you too."

"Heh, most of mine are long gone." He tapped his chest. "But they live in my heart."

"We'll get you back home," Grey Cloak promised.

The wind picked up, blowing dust all over. He closed his eyes and waited for it to pass, pondering. He'd never been close to anyone other than Dyphestive. Even in the dragon kennels of Dark Mountain, he hadn't had friends. Friendship wasn't a virtue of the Riskers. It was considered a weakness. But times had changed, and he had more friends than ever, and it hurt when he lost them. "I'm going to put an end to this war. I swear it."

Nath patted him on the back. "It's good to have goals. Especially noble ones." A shadow passed overhead, and he looked up. "Your leader returns."

Anya and Cinder were landing.

"She's not my leader."

"Well, someone is going to have to be."

As soon as Cinder touched the ground, Anya vaulted out of the saddle and stormed straight toward Grey Cloak, pulling her sword. "Grab some steel. It's time for a lesson!"

Taken aback, he responded, "What?"

"You heard me!" She brushed the hair from her eyes and stuck her sword at him. "If you are too sick in the belly to ride a dragon, then I need to know if you can handle yourself on the ground."

Grey Cloak stood, and without breaking eye contact, he said, "I can handle myself fine." He walked up to the tip of her sword and pushed it away with his finger. "Aren't you being childish?"

"As the last Sky Rider, I am in charge, and you are being insubordinate," Anya said.

"In charge? What gives you the assumption that you are in charge?"

By that time, the other dragons and Dyphestive had landed, and they gathered around at a safe distance.

"As I said, I'm the last—"

"No, you aren't the last. I'm a Sky Rider, too, and so is Dyphestive, because he's a natural too."

Anya turned her attention on Dyphestive, who was standing in Rock's shadow. "Riding a dragon doesn't make him a Sky Rider. There is training, the same as you and I did."

"We don't have time for a Sky Rider school, Anya. You only want it so that you can be everyone's taskmaster. The truth is that you are wasting time. You are delaying."

Anya got nose to nose with him. "I'm not delaying! I'm not wasting time. I'm building an army, and you are getting in the way with your shenanigans!"

"I thought we agreed that we were going to the Wizard Watch. What happened to that?"

"You still don't have a plan, and we still aren't ready."

"I think they're going to kiss," Feather said under her breath.

"No, we aren't!" Grey Cloak and Anya quickly distanced themselves.

She pointed her finger at Grey Cloak and said, "We have to have a leader, and if we can't decide between ourselves, there is only one way to settle it."

"Really?" Grey Cloak crossed his arms. "And what might that be?"

Anya stuck her sword into the ground. "By combat!"

3

Grey Cloak stepped back and chuckled. "You can't be serious."

"Don't I look serious?" Anya unbuckled her sword and tossed it aside then started removing the metal bracers on her wrists. "This is the way of the Sky Riders. One can challenge another for leadership once in a season. This is how my uncle Justus became the last leader of the Sky Riders. He defeated Hogrim on several occasions." She chucked her bracers. "You can back down and let me be the leader."

Grey Cloak caught the eyes of everyone in the audience. Dyphestive scratched the scraggly hairs on his cheek and shrugged.

"Don't you want in on this, brother? You have a right to fight too."

"No, I'll let you fight this fight on your own. I'll be glad to lend my sword to the one that prevails," Dyphestive replied.

"Great." Grey Cloak shrugged and turned his attention back to Anya. "Why are you undressing?"

She'd started wiggling out of her armor. "Oh, did you want to use blades and fight to the death? That's been done before as well." Anya shed her chest plate and set it down. She kept two daggers in each boot, and she tossed those away, followed by another three small blades in her belt and two sharp hair pins. "I think that's all of them. Oh, wait." She'd missed another blade on her thigh. Anya flipped it into the ground between Grey Cloak's feet. "That's the last of them."

Removing his sword belt, he asked, "So, are we going to wrestle?"

"Whoever beats the other into submission first wins." Anya tied her hair in a ponytail. "No weapons, no wizard fire. You can only use the muscle and bone that life gave you."

"Finally, some excitement. I can't wait to see these little people beat the snot out of each other," Fenora stated.

"Stay out of it, daughter," Cinder warned.

"You can whip her, brother," Streak said with his twin tails slowly drumming the ground. "A quick punch to the throat will do her in."

Cinder gave Streak the stink eye and said, "Streak, mind your tongue."

"Sorry, Pops. But you have to let us root for our favorite," Streak said with a sheepish look. "Right?"

Cinder shook his head.

"What are you waiting for?" Anya asked. "Aren't you going to take off that security blanket you live in?"

Grey Cloak narrowed his eyes. He unclasped the cloak at the collar and draped it over Streak's snout. "Take care of this for me." He looked at Anya over his shoulder. "I won't be long."

Back in Dark Mountain, when he was a youth, Grey Cloak had seen more fights between Riskers vying for status and position than he could remember. The same sort of battle went on between fledglings that were going through the ripening too. All of the adepts fought for pride and status. It was encouraged. He'd mopped up many bloodstained floors, not to mention dragging the battered and broken bodies of combatants across them. He'd been trained by the Sky Riders too. Those days had been every bit as brutal and nasty but without the competitive brawling, because he was the only one training.

"Do you want to pat me down?" Grey Cloak lifted his arms and spun around. "I don't carry the same number of weapons that you do."

Anya had removed the last piece of her armor. Her sweat-soaked tunic and buckskin trousers clung to her pleasing build. The firm muscles in her arms and shoulders showed. She eyed him and said, "You'd better not have anything up your sleeve."

"No need to worry." He removed his shirt, revealing layers of hard muscles on a lean frame. "I think it would be best if we talked our way through this."

"We've done enough talking." Anya gave a heavy stare and began to walk around him. "It's going to be either you or me."

"I guess it's going to be me, then," he said without taking his eyes off of her. Even though he had a stronger build than Anya, he didn't doubt for a moment her skill and strength. She was a natural, the same as him. Her abilities were far beyond normal limits. "We need someone to oversee the fight. Who will that be?"

"I'll do it!" Fenora responded.

"No, let me!" Feather said.

Nath sat up from the boulder and lifted a hand. "I'll handle the duties, if both of you agree."

They nodded.

The hermit wandered between them, and with a golden sparkle in his eye, he said, "In a world I once visited, they called a fight such as this a no-holds-barred contest. The combatants battled before the eyes of tens of thousands of spectators. There's nothing more exciting than a battle with life on the line." He eyeballed them both. "This fight will go on until one of you submits... or dies."

Anya gave Grey Cloak a confident look. She pounded

her fist into her palm. "Don't worry. I won't kill you, but by the time I finish, you'll wish you were dead."

He smirked. "We'll see about that."

Nath took them by the wrists and hauled them away from the weapons and into an area of small rocks and sand. He called to the others, "Wall them in. No one leaves until it's over."

Cinder, Rock, and Fenora formed a triangle spaced twenty yards apart. Feather, Streak, and Dyphestive spread out and filled in open spaces between the large gaps.

"Stay inside the triangle," Nath warned. "Otherwise, anything goes inside. Are you ready?"

Grey Cloak and Anya nodded.

Nath backed away and said in a loud voice that hinted at its previous youthful strength, "Then let the rumble begin!"

Anya offered her hand. "May the best natural win."

He reached for her grip.

She hit him square in the jaw. Stars exploded behind his eyes. His knees buckled, and he fell.

4

BEFORE GREY CLOAK hit the ground, Anya had him in a headlock. She drove his head into the dirt and said, "Yield!"

The thought of surrender briefly crossed his mind. With his lips kissing the ground, he struggled to say, "I accept your surrender!"

"I didn't surrender!" Anya cranked up the pressure and squeezed his head tighter. "You surrender!"

Grey Cloak clawed at her forearm and tried to pull it away. "Never," he muttered.

"You're going to regret that decision shortly." Muscles in her arms bunched, and she began to choke him to death.

Nath took a knee beside them and said, "He has to submit on his own. Choking him out won't garner victory if he's not alive to speak it."

Anya gave Nath a fiery look and said, "Fine. I'll try something else." She scissor-locked Grey Cloak's legs in hers, released his head, put him in a submission arm bar, and leaned back.

"Aaargh!" Grey Cloak screamed at the top of his lungs. He'd spent the majority of his life avoiding hard work and unwanted melee. He relied on cunning and speed instead of straight-up fighting, and he was paying for that lack of balance. He gave Anya a look of pain.

Her face was lit up in triumph. "Submit to me!" she said. "Submit before I rip your arm off!"

She's out of her skull!

With pain shooting through his arm and burning into his shoulder, he scanned the faces that made up the triangle. The dragons of Safe Haven returned hard-eyed stares. He could see in their eyes that they were waiting for him to give in at any moment. They saw him defeated before the fight had barely started. It ignited a fire inside him.

Who are they to doubt me? They don't even know me.

Streak's broad skull came into view. One of his bright-yellow eyes winked, and his pink tongue flicked.

Grey Cloak's eyes locked with Dyphestive's as he writhed on the ground. His brother's thick arms were crossed over his broad chest. He returned Grey Cloak's stare with a confident nod.

The fire inside his belly started to spread. He lifted his

shoulders from the ground and looked at Anya, and through clenched teeth, he said, "You want a fight? You got it!"

She leaned back farther, amping up the pressure, and said, "I've got you, all right!"

The moment she leaned back to pull his arm out of its socket, he lifted his legs over his head and flipped flat onto his belly. At the same time, he jerked and twisted free of her strong grip. He rolled away and bounced to his feet.

Anya jumped to her feet. "You squirm like a worm. No surprise."

He wiped the blood from the corner of his mouth with his fingers and looked at it, rubbing it between his finger and thumb. "You caught me off guard once. It won't happen again."

"Hah! I don't need the element of surprise to defeat you. You might squirm, but you can't fight."

"We'll see about that."

"Stop talking and start dancing!" Fenora bellowed. "I want to see some action!"

Anya leaped five feet off of the ground and descended on Grey Cloak.

He was ready that time. With a quick side step, he slid away from her attack and slipped in behind her.

Anya launched a back kick into his gut.

"Oof!" He doubled over just in time to catch a bone-rattling roundhouse kick to the face. He collapsed to the ground.

Anya pounced on the backs of his knees and started whaling on him in a flurry of hard fists.

"Get him! Get him!" Fenora chanted.

"Your blood brother isn't a very skilled fighter," Rock said to Dyphestive.

"I've seen butterflies put up a better fight than that," Fenora added.

In the wink of an eye, Grey Cloak was eating dirt again. Anya hammered him in the back. She wasn't holding back anything. The moment she stopped hitting him, she went for a headlock. He feigned defeat, and a moment before she could get him by the neck, he scrambled away like a frightened rabbit. Back on his feet, he turned and faced her, huffing and puffing.

Anya sat on her knees, fists on hips, glowering up at him. "You are a coward. You have no business leading the Sky Riders or anyone." She put her hands behind her back and lifted her chin. "Come closer. I'll give you a free strike."

"Do it, master," Streak urged him. "Take the fight to her."

Grey Cloak swallowed. His body was covered in sweat and sandy grit, and he hadn't even landed a punch. "Rise, Anya. If I'm going to defeat you, I'll do it on the square."

She stood. "You're going to wish you'd at least got a shot in once this is over."

He shrugged. "We'll see how it goes." He lifted his fists and cracked his neck from side to side. "Besides, I'm all warmed up now."

5

THE BATTLE ENSUED, with Anya on the attack and Grey Cloak dancing away, looking for an opening. She came at him like a charging bull with blood in her eyes. Her attacks were skilled and precise, fluid and powerful.

Boy, did I underestimate her.

He blocked a punch with his hands and jumped away from a side kick.

Anya had been a battle-hardened fighter before he'd met her and a Sky Rider of at least ten years, and she had been spending her time in hiding training for the next big fight. His life wasn't even twenty seasons.

"Come on, little man. Fight her!" Fenora barked. "Either that, or give up!"

With the dragon egging him on, Grey Cloak launched

his own flurry of attacks. He jabbed, blocked, and countered with a kick to Anya's ribs. She staggered, off balance.

"That's how you do it!" Fenora said.

Using his feet for weapons, Grey Cloak unleashed an aerial assault of scissor kicks.

Anya backed away, ducking and blocking. Her heated stare never left his.

He saw an opening and aimed a kick for her head.

Anya went high to block with her arms.

Perfect.

Grey Cloak adjusted his leg attack, dropped low, and swept her legs, which flew out from underneath her. She landed flat on her back, and her head bounced off of the ground.

I've got her. He jumped in behind her and went for the same headlock she'd put him in earlier.

Pain exploded in his nose. *Crack!*

Anya had busted him in the face with her knuckles. The audience oohed.

"Nice try," Anya said in a stone-cold voice.

Grey Cloak bled from the nose. It must have been broken, and spots were in his eyes. On his knees, he lost sight of her for a moment.

Shake it off!

In a sudden turn of events, Anya grabbed him by the hair, pulled him up, and started punching him in the belly.

The punishment didn't stop there. She clubbed his head with a few hard shots and drove her knee into his chin.

He lay on his back, looking into the sun-glazed sky only for her face to interfere.

"You need to surrender," she said.

"No," he groaned. He sluggishly rolled over to his hands and knees then looked up at her and said, "You need to surrender while I'm still showing mercy."

Anya kicked him in the ribs.

"Oof!"

The battle continued.

Anya beat Grey Cloak from one corner of the arena to another. His face swelled. His bones ached.

She wrangled him to the ground, only to see him slip away from her grip like a greased pig. She chased him down and knocked him down again.

Every so often, Grey Cloak slipped in a few rabbit punches. He headbutted her chin once, but that made his skull ache more. He tripped her a time or two, and red-faced, she made him pay for it.

He caught the eyes of the onlookers. They appeared embarrassed for him. Fenora shook her head. Feather looked away. Rock's stare was as heavy and impersonal as always. Cinder's bright eyes showed compassion.

As Grey Cloak crawled away from Anya's clutches, she stepped on his back. "Will you quit? You are embarrassing yourself."

"Me? Embarrassed?" He squirted out from under her foot and propped himself up on his elbows. "I've never felt better," he said, panting.

"You are no match for me!" she replied through clenched teeth. "Surrender, and I'll show mercy."

"Never surrender," he mumbled as he fought his way back to his feet. He raised his fists. "Besides, I still like my chances."

He heard some members of the audience groan. He lifted his hands and shrugged at them.

"You are outmatched, Grey Cloak. Yield to me so that we can move forward," Anya demanded.

He shook his head.

She narrowed her eyes. "You'll regret this." She charged forward and tackled him to the ground. Her fists dug into his ribs, and she forced his head down and made him eat dirt.

As slippery as an eel, Grey Cloak escaped and danced backward on wobbly legs. He swayed in his fighting stance and beckoned her on with one fist. "Come on."

An endless flurry of kicks, punches, hip tosses, and leg sweeps followed. The fight, which should have ended quickly, went on and on and on.

They were naturals with stamina beyond that of mere mortals. But even they could tire—eventually.

An hour passed. Anya drubbed Grey Cloak without

ceasing. He limbed, hopped. crawled, fell, and battled back again. He took her best and suffered the worst.

The longer it went on, the angrier Anya became. She lifted Grey Cloak over her head and slammed him to the ground. "Surrender!"

He lay sprawled out on his back and shook his head. "I'm still warming up."

Cinder's head went down, and the grand dragon sighed.

Anya stood over Grey Cloak with her chest heaving behind her sweat-soaked jerkin. Her swollen hand trembled when she wiped the damp strands of hair from her eyes. "You are going to die if you don't yield."

"I'll die before I ever give in to you." He came to his feet like rising smoke and smirked. "Besides, I've been saving my energy."

"For what?" she asked with a shaky voice. "Losing?"

"No, this." He struck like a cobra, planting a kick in her gut that doubled her over. In a moment, he let loose a violent assault of punches and kicks that Anya couldn't recover from. *Whop! Bap! Bap! Bap! Whoom!*

He tied up one hand in her ponytail and used his free fist to beat her. His reserved strength matched his speed, which was what he'd been waiting for. He'd let her tire herself out and turned all of his fire on.

Anya's counters were good but not good enough. He beat her to the punch, the kick, and the trip. Grey Cloak put her on her backside, watched her scramble up, and knocked her down again. He didn't let up. Her strength dried up. She bled, gasping, and collapsed.

Grey Cloak put a knee in her back and locked his arm around her neck. "It's over, Anya. You've exhausted yourself, and I'm full of wind. It's time that you surrendered."

She shook her head. "Never!"

Grey Cloak increased the pressure. Her neck muscles were like cords of iron, and her strength was like a wild boar's. But she was sapped. He could feel it. "Yield, Anya. Yield."

She pushed up to one knee. Her body shook all over as she rose from the ground, then she collapsed. With a disgruntled sigh, she tapped his forearm and nodded.

"Anya yields!" Nath called. He put his hand on Grey Cloak's shoulder. "Let her go."

Grey Cloak loosened his aching arms. A sea of black assailed him, and he passed out.

6

HIGH ROCK

THE JAGGED PINNACLES of High Rock threatened to pierce the clouds. The sheer cliffs of rock were called the Shards from the Heavens by the sky gnomes. Their legends said that the gods had battled in the heavens, and the great sheets of rocks were chips from stars that were used as weapons.

Zora half believed the tall tale as she gazed across the field of rocks, which appeared to be dropped from the sky and sunk into the dry land. She stood on an overlook, surveying the surrounding cliffs of her strange abode. The sky gnomes, smallish men with large hands, large eyes, and fuzzy ears, remained busy marching along rope bridges that connected spire to spire.

From time to time, the gnomes jetted through the air on

the backs of great vultures, gliding through the tall rocks and disappearing.

Zora tightened her wool blanket over her shoulders. With the icy winds whistling through the crags, she'd spent days observing the hundreds of gnomes that scurried in the rocks like ants on a hill. The rocks' pinnacles were laden with caves and notches where the gnomes lived and their vultures nested. No matter the time of the day, they were always on the move.

"Aren't you cold?" Razor asked. The savvy sword master approached with a limp from the warmth of the cave behind her. He wore his battered suit of black leather armor, which still had blood caked on it. He stood beside her and gazed into the beyond. "Or tired?"

"We need to leave." Her jaw clenched. "It's been days, and they keep holding us here."

Razor leaned over the precipice, and in his charming, rugged voice said, "It's a long way down. And you know me. I'm not much for climbing."

Durmost the sky gnome had taken them to a pinnacle that was not connected by rope bridges like the others. It was a lone tower of stone—a prison. The trek down was almost vertical and well over one thousand feet. Even for Zora, the climb would be harrowing.

"What do you suppose that we do? Wait here?" Zora asked. "It's been days since Durmost abandoned us here. I have a feeling we aren't guests. What about you?"

Razor shook the clay jug in his hand, the watery contents sloshing. "Their wine isn't the best, but I've had worse dragon spit. My wounds are healing, and my belly's full. I can think of a worse situation to be in." He offered her the bottle. "Why don't you have a swig? Loosen up while the going is good."

She turned her nose away. Even though Durmost and the sky gnomes had saved them from a certain fiery death, her stomach still twisted. Crane, Jakoby, and Leena were gone—dead gone. The guilt of their deaths sat like a lump in the pit of her stomach, and she couldn't shake it. "I want to be left alone."

Razor glanced over his shoulder into the mouth of the cave where they were staying. "They didn't leave us with separate caves. I couldn't leave you alone if I had to." He looked down. "But I could jump if you like."

"Not funny."

Gorva joined them. The tall orcen woman's hair was braided, and she wore a new suit of buckskin clothing that the sky gnomes had provided for her. "Is Razor bothering you again?"

"Apparently, I'm bothering everybody. Sorry." He hurled the jug into the sky and wandered back into the cave. "But don't come crying to me when you get lonely."

Gorva crossed her arms, sat on the rock wall of the overlook, and said, "I take it you're still feeling guilty."

"More than ever." Zora could still see the flames of

Steelhammer engulfing her friends. "I should have been able to stop it with the dragon charm."

"Hella and her dragon were powerful. We are fortunate that any of us survived." Gorva looked over her shoulder. Her eyes followed the giant vultures soaring through the air. "We won't let their sacrifice be for nothing."

Zora scowled. "Huh. It's all been for nothing. Look at us. We're the only ones left, and we don't have any idea where Grey Cloak and Dyphestive are. They are probably captured or dead too."

"Don't be negative. It's not like you. Be strong."

Zora's frown deepened.

"When was the last time you checked for the Medallion of Location that Grey Cloak carries?" Gorva asked.

With a heavy-hearted sigh, Zora moved away from Gorva and stopped in front of a stone table where Crane's satchel lay. She picked it up and removed the small jewelry box–shaped container. When they'd first arrived in High Rock, she checked it every hour, only to wind up seeing nothing. It became too depressing to check on a routine basis, so she'd set it aside. Without looking, she set it on the table and opened it up. "Feel free to look for yourself. I can't bear it."

Gorva pushed off of the wall as Zora walked away.

Staring into the box, Gorva asked, "What are we looking to see?"

"A green dot, like a burning flame in a sea of black sand."

"And you don't see it?" Gorva asked.

Zora had her back turned. "No."

"I see a green speck in the sands."

Zora turned and raised an eyebrow. "I'd expect a jest from Razor but not you. You aren't toying with me?"

"I think you know me well enough by now to know that I don't have a strong sense of humor." Gorva held the box outward. "Come look for yourself."

With a doubtful expression, Zora sauntered over to Gorva and dropped her gaze on the box. As clear as the sky, a green speck sat at the edge of the box. Her head snapped up. "That's it! That's it!"

"What do we do?" Gorva asked.

"Durmost told us if we needed anything to wave." She ran to the overlook and lifted her hands. "Start waving!"

7

———

"I SEE this speck that you speak of, but I don't understand its importance," Durmost said. The older gnome's face was a mask of concentration as he sat on the table with the jewel box in his hand. He dangled his short legs over the edge, kicking them like a child. With a clack, he closed the lid and handed the box to Zora. "And it's of no consequence at the moment. You have to be seen by Jumax first."

"You've been saying that for days," Zora reminded the fuzzy-eared gnome. "It's imperative that we join up with our friends. They are looking for us, and we are looking for them."

Durmost hopped off of the table and looked up at her. "You owe the sky gnomes a life debt. You cannot leave until you repay it."

Zora exchanged confused looks with Gorva, whose brow was knitted, and with Razor, who stood at the overlook, trying to avoid the giant vulture that followed his every move like a hawk.

Gorva grabbed the gnome by his vest and lifted him. "What is this life debt that you speak of?" She shook him. "This is the first we've heard of it."

"Jumax decides the life debt. He will tell you when he is ready." Durmost eyeballed Gorva's arms. "I am a sky gnome commander. Do you know the penalty for assaulting a sky gnome commander?" he asked in his spirited voice.

"No, but do you know what will happen when I throw you out of this cave? Do you think your ugly bird will be fast enough to catch you before you hit the earth?"

Durmost's bright expression deflated, and he said, "Since you are guests, I'll let your transgression pass."

"Guests!" Razor moved away from the vulture that stalked him. "More like prisoners. Durmost, call your thing off of me. It's creepy."

"You didn't complain when we saved you. A life for a life," Durmost said.

"Put him down," Zora said with defeat.

Gorva planted Durmost on the table.

Durmost straightened his leather vest, which was decorated with bird feathers, and said, "Jumax will deal with your situation. He decides your next path and how you will repay your life debt." He held out his oversized hands and offered a broad smile. "When that is settled, you can go."

The vulture had Razor cornered inside the cave. Its beak was pressed against his face. "Durmost, if you don't call off your buzzard, I'm going to gut it."

"The crime for slaughtering our sacred ones is death," Durmost said politely. "I would suggest that you don't do that. Besides, I think she likes you."

"She?" Razor's eyebrows wiggled. "That's one ugly *she*." He squeezed out from the vulture and hid behind Gorva. "Protect me."

Gorva shook her head.

Zora pleaded with Durmost. "Will you please tell Jumax that it is urgent that we join our friends as soon as possible? I beg of you, Durmost."

"Jumax hears your plea. But he must prioritize his responsibilities."

Zora sighed as she twisted her hair around her finger. She wanted to poke Durmost's eyes out. The gnome was driving her crazy. She could only imagine how difficult it would be to deal with another one just like him.

"Don't you like your accommodations? The food? Eh? The drink?" Durmost asked. "You are being treated well, yes?"

"Yes, but you don't understand. We need to join our friends. They are in danger. We have to help them."

"Tell me more about this danger," Durmost said.

Zora, Gorva, and Razor let out simultaneous sighs. They'd spoken in detail about the Dragon Wars and Black Frost on more than one occasion. For whatever reason, the story hadn't sunk in with Durmost.

"Never mind," Zora said quietly.

A loud shriek of a bird carried into the cave.

Durmost leaped from the table and hurried to the cave's overlook. He pointed into the sky. "Jumax! You are blessed!"

"What in the world is that?" Razor asked as the group moved outside of the cave.

A great creature, like a middling dragon but with the head, feathers, and wings of a bird, soared through the sky and shrieked again.

"That's a griffon," Durmost said. "Beautiful, isn't he?"

A man rode on the back of the flying beast. He sat tall in the saddle, broad and muscular.

"That's Jumax? I thought he was a gnome," Zora said.

"No, Jumax is not a gnome. Jumax is Jumax," Durmost replied.

The griffon soared high overhead, and Jumax leaped from the saddle. He spread his great wings and sailed right toward them.

"He comes!" Durmost said as he backed away. "Jumax comes. Clear the way!"

Everyone cleared the deck as Jumax descended upon them in a dive. At the last moment, he pulled up his wings, turned his body upward, and landed softly on the ledge as gently as a bird. He said in an engaging and commanding voice, "I am Jumax. Durmost, introduce me to our guests."

8

Zora's blood warmed under Jumax's heavy gaze. He was one of the most handsome men she'd ever seen. His head was shaved clean, and the brown skin on his muscular chest and arms glistened. He stood taller than Gorva and was almost as broad as Dyphestive but showed more well-defined muscle.

She extended her hand, which trembled slightly, and said, "I'm Gorva... I mean, I'm Zora."

Jumax clasped her small hand in both of his and kissed it. "It is my pleasure to meet you, Zora." His feathers were like a raiment that moved like the wings of a bird. His primitive dress was unique, no more than a loincloth of feathers and sandals with high straps around the ankles. In addition to his hawkish good looks, he carried a fashionable sword and a dagger with bird-head pommels in the decorated sheaths in his sword belt. His bare legs were like tree trunks knotted in muscle that flexed when he turned his attention to Gorva. The man stretched his hands to Gorva and asked, "And you are?"

"Gorva," she replied with a dry throat. She cleared it and said again more clearly, "Gorva."

Zora was surprised that the hardened orcen warrior let Jumax kiss her hands with his full lips. It appeared that Gorva was as smitten as she was.

Razor offered his hand. "I'm Reginald the Razor. Blade master."

Jumax had to tear his gaze from Gorva and Zora and shook Razor's hand with little effort. "Nice to meet you." He let go.

"What? No kiss?" Razor quipped.

Zora rocked on her heels, cleared her throat, and said, "Uh, Jumax, we have certainly enjoyed your hospitality, but it is imperative that we leave."

With his eyes fixed on Gorva he said, "No, you won't be leaving. You owe me a life debt. Such a debt is not easily repaid." His nostrils flared as he studied Gorva and put his large hands on her shoulders. "Perhaps we can work something out, if this matter is *truly* urgent."

Zora said, "It is—"

Jumax cut her off with a wave of his hand. "My faithful commander Durmost has informed me about your situation. I am well aware of Black Frost and his minions. But we have no war with Black Frost in the south. We live peacefully."

"For now," Razor said. "Peace never lasts if you aren't willing to fight for it."

"Little man, I know more about fighting than you'll ever know." Jumax cupped Gorva's face. "Your beauty is unique. I've never seen the likes of it."

Zora could have sworn that Gorva blushed underneath her ruddy skin. The orc woman gently pulled Jumax's hand away. "Jumax, you should listen to them. To us."

Jumax tilted his head to one side and caressed Gorva's cheek with the back of his hand. "You are a natural, aren't you?"

"Yes," Gorva said. "I am the daughter of Hogrim the Sky Rider."

Jumax tossed his head back and let out a gusty laugh. "A daughter of a Sky Rider! How intriguing." He rubbed his cheek and raised an eyebrow. "How is it that a natural came to be in the company of inferior beings?"

Razor drew his shoulders back. "Whoa, fella. Where do you get off calling your guests inferior?"

Jumax waved him off. "Don't take it personally, little man. If you had been born a natural, you would understand." He gave Razor a threatening gaze. "And I'd be wary of insulting your host, who could bend your swords around your neck."

"I'd like to see you—"

Gorva slapped Razor in the shoulder and asked, "So, you are a natural too?"

"You seem surprised, young beauty. Didn't your father ever tell you that not all naturals ride the skies on the backs of great lizards?" Jumax chuckled. "There are other sorts of naturals, such as me, that ride on the backs of griffons."

"I never knew," Gorva replied.

"Pfft! Of course you didn't. And it's no surprise. The Sky Riders treat naturals such as me like we're dragon dung." His face darkened, and his voice did too. "Oh yes, the mighty Sky Riders, soaring on their dragons like they're the gods of the air. Ha, look at them now. So prideful and vain. Now they're all dead."

"That's my father that you speak about," Gorva said with a snarl.

"And your father's life ended in a fiery grave created by the flames of Black Frost. I know about it." He gestured to Durmost and the thriving sky society beyond the cave. "We all know about it." He put both hands on Gorva's shoulders. "Let me tell you about your father and the likes of him. I don't question their bravery, and I admired their sense of duty, but before Black Frost rose to the heights of his power, we offered our assistance to the Sky Riders. We wanted to fight alongside them on the Day of Betrayal. The fools said they didn't need us. They laughed at our giant beasts of the sky and the earth. They thought their self-righteousness would see their great efforts through." He scoffed. "But they failed. And Black Frost's power is thus that it can never be defeated."

Gorva slipped away from his hands and said, "Surely you don't believe that."

"Oh, but I do. After all, if the Sky Riders can't defeat him, then how can the likes of us?"

Zora put her small hand on his muscular arm and said, "By not making the same mistakes as they did."

Jumax gave her a serious look and replied, "Wisdom and beauty—a rare gift. Durmost, bring them to my spire, and I'll explain to them how the life debt can be repaid." He kissed the hands of both Zora and Gorva, moved to the overlook, bent at the knees, and launched into the sky. He plummeted toward the ground and landed easily in the saddle of his griffon then flew away.

"I'll give him one thing. He sure knows how to make an entrance," Razor admitted. "And an exit. Say, how do you gals think I'd look in a feather loincloth and wings?"

9

WIZARD WATCH

TATIANA STOOD behind Lord Verbard in the Time Mural chamber. The silver-eyed underling stood over the pedestal of gemstones and was busy arranging them in different orders. Lord Catten stood on one of the twin pewter thrones behind them, drinking from a golden chalice. His golden eyes were as bright as coins as he stared into the massive archway that contained the Time Mural, which was as black as space at the moment.

"Do I need to arrange the stones again?" Lord Catten quipped. He took a sip of a dark wine called port and sucked through his sharp teeth. His black robes rustled when he moved, and the gray skin of his round face was drawn tight in a grimace of evil. In the grip of his other hand was the Star of Light, a bright stone. His sharp black fingernails tapped the stone's surface. "We've been at this long enough. It's time to move on."

Lord Verbard looked over his shoulder and said, "You are more than welcome to try, but you'll only overcomplicate matters, as you always do."

"Pfft," Lord Catten said with an eye roll.

Tatiana kept her eyes averted. The last time she'd stared into Lord Verbard's eyes, he almost burned her mind out. The underlings had powers that she didn't comprehend, and they wielded them without mercy. She'd been their minion for years, toiling by their sides, working at their demanding beck and call. Her body ached. She was tired beyond reason and fought to keep her eyes open. Her vibrant skin had turned ashen, and the locks of her lustrous hair had thinned.

"Open a door. Anything," Lord Catten demanded.

Lord Verbard's feet lifted off of the floor, and his stark ebony robes dragged beneath him. "We are increasing the size of the portal, are we not? Or do you want to send one of these minions on another journey?"

"The portal is large enough," Lord Catten said with a hiss.

"Black Frost wants it as large as possible," Lord Verbard replied.

Lord Catten sawed his finger under his black lips and said, "He won't know the difference. The portal is more than large enough for a grand dragon to waltz through.

Two of them could squeeze through side by side." He turned his burning gaze on Tatiana. "What do you think, woman?"

She could feel heat on her back. Tatiana swallowed the lump in her throat, turned toward him, and said, "Agreed, Lord Catten."

Lord Catten opened his arms, leaned forward, and said, "See? That is good enough for me. This woman knows. Now, go and fetch one of your minions from the dungeons." He picked up a dark glass bottle that sat on a small ornate table beside his throne and shook it. "And bring along another bottle from the wine cellar."

"As you wish." Tatiana bowed before both underlings and hurried out of the chamber. She didn't stop walking until the sound of their harsh bickering voices was gone. She entered an alcove that led from tower level to tower level and went inside a shaft that used magic to drop down from level to level. On her way down, she covered her face, sobbed deeply, and sank to the floor.

"Tatiana," someone said softly.

At first, she thought she was hearing things. Sleep deprivation and starvation had made her delusional more than once. She peeked through her fingers and saw the shimmering form of Dalsay. With a shaky voice, she asked, "Is it really you, my love?"

Dalsay knelt his ghostly form beside her and said, "It is I, my love."

She choked out a sob and said, "I wish I could touch you." She reached out and palmed his cheek. A faint warmth passed into her hand. "It is you." She started to cry uncontrollably. "Where have you been?"

"I found them," he said in a low voice. "Grey Cloak and Dyphestive live. They have retrieved the Figurine of Heroes."

She wiped the tears from her face and started to rise. "You swear it?"

"I do," Dalsay said with a nod.

Her blood warmed, and her back straightened. "Is the tower still guarded by Black Frost's armies?"

Dalsay nodded. "And the elves comb the surrounding lands as well. It will be difficult to get the brothers and the figurine inside."

"No, it will be impossible. The underlings have prepared for everything. The towers are filled with wards and traps, even if they make it inside. And only a wizard can let them in. It has to be me or you or Gossamer."

Dalsay shook his head. "You can't tell anyone about me. It is too risky. Tell me... what are the underlings trying to accomplish with the Time Mural?"

Tatiana braced her back against the wall and caught her breath. Her heart was racing. Dalsay had given her better news than she could have ever hoped for. "They are still mastering the Time Mural, but I fear that they are close. They have opened portals to other worlds as well as this one, but they can't control it. They've sent many of our brethren through the portal, but they have yet to return. The last man almost made it, but his body was destroyed." She took another breath. "And they are making the portal bigger for Black Frost. I believe he wants to summon an army from another world."

"Or flee to another to conquer once he has destroyed this one. His appetite for power is bottomless."

"The underlings' ambitions are as great as his," she said. "I believe they are trying to do his bidding and, at the same time, return to their world."

The shaft came to a stop.

"I need to go," she said with a worried look. "They count every second that I do anything. When the time comes, I'll do what I can to help get the Figurine of Heroes inside. But I don't see how."

Dalsay offered a warm smile and tried to touch her face. "In the words of our friend Grey Cloak, 'I'll think of something.'"

10

CINDER WADED into the silvery waters of a lake inside Safe Haven. His body was fully immersed, with only his head rising above the water. He drank a mouthful and eyed Anya. She sat at the top of the bank, arms wrapped around her knees, staring out over the water.

"You've been very quiet of late," Cinder said.

Anya didn't reply. She looked away from his probing gaze and picked mustard-yellow moss from the ground. Her face was swollen, and she had bruises all over.

"I can't believe he beat me," she muttered.

Cinder stretched his head toward her, tilted his horns, and asked, "What was that?"

She glowered at him. "You heard me."

"I suppose I did. You need to move on, Anya. There are

more important matters that we need to attend to. You are needed," he said.

She slowly shook her head. "In a year, I'll challenge him again. He won't trick me another time."

Cinder lay his head on the bank and sighed. His hot breath stirred her locks of hair. "Anya, you can't stew for a year and challenge him again. The time to act is now. And you need to be a part of that."

"We should leave. He can command the dragons and train the Sky Riders himself. As if he knows anything about training anyone. He only serves himself."

"You're being childish."

Cinder's words stung her heart. "How can you take his side?"

"I'm not taking a side. I'm being a friend," he said politely.

"I don't need a friend that tells me how wrong I am!" she shouted. "I need a friend on my side! Why don't you go away, Cinder? Go and play with your children!"

Cinder gave her a hurt look. He slunk away and vanished under the water, which bubbled, surged up the bank, and mellowed into gentle waves until it flattened out again.

Anya blew the hair from her eyes. The long lock dropped back to the same place. She pulled a dagger, cut off the lock, and slung it toward the water. "There!"

"Brutal. Plain brutal," Nath said in his scratchy voice and ambled over.

"You. Are you eavesdropping, hermit?" she asked in a bitter voice. "Or spying for Grey Cloak?"

"No one pays attention to a hermit. It's a difficult thing for me to get used to." He sat down beside her. "You should treat your hair better. It won't always be so full and thick." He ran his claw-like scaly fingers through his stringy hair. "Trust one who knows. Why, I had a glorious mane of hair unlike anything you've ever seen. As wild as flame. It made your beautiful strands—"

"Did I ask you to sit with me?" She scooted away.

"I wasn't looking for permission." Nath nodded toward the lake. "I overheard your heated exchange with Cinder. You weren't so kind to him."

"He'll get over it. It's not the first time he's seen me brood before." She stabbed her dagger into the ground and looked at Nath. "Let me guess. You came to offer me your sage advice."

"Very perceptive."

"Well, you can take your wise musings and stick them where the sun doesn't shine." She got up, plucked her dagger from the ground, and pointed it at him. "Or I can stick something else where the sun won't shine."

Nath chuckled. "You really are a firecracker. And I'd be careful where you point that dagger. It would be a shame if you underestimated another opponent again."

She slammed the dagger into its sheath and said, "What is that supposed to mean?"

"You wonder why you lost?" He started to rise and groaned as he did so. "My knees feel awful. Anyway..." He cleared his throat. "I'll tell you why you lost." He reached out and tapped her forehead. "You thought you were the better fighter. Decades of training. And you have years of experience on him. Right? He's not even twenty seasons, and you're well over thirty. He's a child, and you are a grown woman. A true warrior." He got nose to nose with her. "All of that gives you the edge—a superior edge. But that doesn't matter if you are lacking one thing."

Her brow knitted. "What am I lacking? I prepare every day." She pushed him back. "I've mastered all that I have been taught."

"There are some matters that you cannot be taught, and that is why you lost."

Her jaw muscles clenched. So did her fists. "If you are implying that he has more heart than I have, I swear I'll bust your nose."

"As long as you don't cut my hair, I'll live. I'm still proud of what I have left. But I'm in desperate need of a blowout."

"You say the strangest things."

"It carries over from strange places."

Anya lifted her eyes upward and sighed. "I don't want to play guessing games with you. Are you going to tell me what it is, or am I supposed to figure it out for myself?"

"Are you asking?"

She crossed her arms and tapped her foot. "Yes."

"Yes, what?"

"Yes, please."

Nath smiled. "Ask and ye shall receive. You share the same weakness as other Sky Riders. It is what Grey Cloak has that you do not. Vision."

"Vision?"

"That is why he beat you. He was three steps ahead before the battle even started. He saw the end result and suffered for it."

Anya's shoulders deflated as she let Nath's words sink into her gut like a great stone. She found a place to sit down. "It all makes sense. I don't know why, but I understand it."

"You've been enlightened."

She nodded. "Perhaps."

"This is a good matter." Nath turned and started to walk away.

"Wait!" she said. "I don't have vision?"

Nath faced her. "You do, Anya, but your pride blinded it."

11

Grey Cloak approached Dyphestive, who was huddled over a basin of water inside the armory, and asked, "What are you doing?"

Dyphestive's bare arms flexed as he wrung water out of a dyed-blue leather hood-like mask of Ghost the Doom Rider. "I'm cleaning these vile things in case we decide to wear them."

Grey Cloak nodded. "I see."

"Hang that up somewhere, will you?" Dyphestive tossed the mask to Grey Cloak.

Holding the hood out in full display, Grey Cloak studied the contorted design of the ugly skull mask. It was a simple device used to strike terror into the hearts of men, and it had proved effective. He remembered terror coursing through his veins the first time he encountered them. It gave a chill that he would never forget. With a frown, he hung the blue mask on the end of a spear that was secured on one of the weapon racks. "Are you well?"

With a shrug of his oversize shoulders, Dyphestive replied, "Never better. How about you and, you know…" He looked toward the mouth of the vault. "Anya?"

"We haven't spoken." Grey Cloak rubbed his hands over the bandages that braced his sore ribs. "And I don't think she's in the mood for talking. I've been looking over my shoulder, waiting for her to jump out from the rocks and attack at any moment."

"She's mad. I'm certain of that." Dyphestive squeezed water out of Scar's red mask. Large drops rained on the toes of his boots. "If you are the leader, you'll need to mend that bridge."

Grey Cloak nodded. "If it can be mended." He caught the flimsy red hood and hung it beside the blue one. "I'll do my best." He saw concern in his brother's face. "I promise." He took a spear from the rack and offered it to Dyphestive for Shamrok's green mask. "You know, there was a time when Anya and I got along quite well. When our search took us to Looseboot. She can be charming when she wants to."

"I don't have any doubt about that."

"Remember the first time we met her? You said you'd marry her."

Dyphestive tried to fight off an embarrassed smile. "That was a long time ago."

"That was only a few years ago, if that. So smitten you were. Imagine what would happen if Leena knew."

"We need to find them. It's not fair that we hide in here and they are trapped out there."

"They are very capable. I'm certain they're well. And the farther from us, the better. After all, we are the source of all of the troubles." He put the spear back on the rack. "Come on. We have plans to make. How about we take another look in the Eye of the Sky Riders. Who knows. Maybe the war has come to an end."

Dyphestive flung the water off of his fingers and followed Grey Cloak deeper into the vault. They gathered by the marble pedestal that housed the Eye of the Sky Riders. He slid away the silk sheet that covered the pedestal and let it gather on the ground.

They stared into the black field, and when Grey Cloak touched the surface, a high aerial view of Gapoli appeared.

Using his fingers, Grey Cloak altered the picture by scanning over leagues of acreage in moments. With his face aglow in the soft light of the image, he asked, "Care to give it a try?"

"I'd love to." Dyphestive began manipulating the image. He zoomed in on rich farmland north of Lake Flugen, where orc farmers were toiling in their fields. "Those were the days."

"Speak for yourself. I think you might be the only man on Gapoli who enjoyed working the soil."

"You have to admit that it was a simpler way to live." Dyphestive moved the image toward Arrowwood, where the land was full of rolling hills rich in streams and bountiful harvests. The images crossed over the Great River into the Wild, where they scanned a few hundred feet above the roads. "Look at that."

At least one thousand elven soldiers were marching west in a neat column. They were in full armor, which consisted of light suits of chain mail and heavier plating on the knees and shoulders. They wore no helmets but carried bows and spears, and every soldier wore a sword belt.

Grey Cloak spread his hands around the edge of the pedestal and leaned closer to the image. "They look like the same soldiers that guarded the Wizard Watch. Why would they be leaving?"

"Perhaps they relieved another legion."

"Possibly, or it might be the opportunity we're looking for." He rolled his finger and said, "Move over the Wizard Watch."

Dyphestive's fingers dusted over the surface. The image moved over the wild forests that surrounded the Wizard Watch. He zoomed out and let the image hover over the land.

Riskers soared through the air on the backs of their dragons. A ring of Black Guard soldiers surrounded the base of the Wizard Watch tower. Another ring of Black Guard soldiers surrounded them, but that was the last line of defense.

"The elves are gone!" Grey Cloak said with wide eyes. "Perhaps they're letting their guard down." He pointed at the skies. "And look. Only one grand dragon is patrolling the skies, leading the middlings." He looked at Dyphestive. "I smell opportunity."

"Maybe their defenses have thinned, but we will still need to find a way in. We'll need a wizard for that."

Grey Cloak drummed his fingers on the pedestal. "We'll have to find one between here and there."

Dyphestive raised an eyebrow. "And if we don't?"

"I'll think of something."

12

"We're taking the dragons?" Anya asked. "I don't think that's wise."

"I believe that speed is of the essence," Grey Cloak replied.

He, Dyphestive, Anya, and Nath had gathered inside the mouth of the Sky Riders' vault, and they'd been discussing his plans, with many of the dragons waiting outside.

"We need to make a move and do it now, or we might miss out on an opportunity," he continued.

Anya paced with her hands behind her back. Her head was down, and she seemed to be having trouble looking at him. "If we lose the dragons, we lose everything."

"We aren't taking all of the dragons. Only ones that we can travel discreetly with," he said.

Anya looked at Cinder and swung her gaze back to Grey Cloak. "Are you suggesting that I don't fly with Cinder?"

"Smaller would be better."

"And if we encounter a grand dragon, we might as well be eaten alive! I won't be separating from Cinder. We are bonded. It's no different from you and Streak. Is it?"

Grey Cloak met her steely gaze. "I'm not going to insist that you come. But I want you to come... and Cinder. However, I didn't want to put the larger dragons at risk."

"I can manage," Cinder said with a nod. "Anya and I have adapted to hiding quite well."

Fenora spoke up. "I don't see why the big dragons can't go. We should go at least part of the way. We need experience too."

"I agree, but we'll start with the smaller dragons that are faster. If we're caught, we'll need to flee quickly," Grey Cloak said. "But first things first. We need the services of a wizard, because we don't know the whereabouts of Dalsay. Anya, you mentioned earlier that you knew one that might be able to help. Care to elaborate?"

"I know of one that might be helpful. He aided Cinder and me once before by a chance encounter. He's not one bred in the towers. He's... different," she said.

"Different how?"

Anya shrugged. "You'll understand when you meet him,

but he won't meet with you without me." She smirked. "And he likes Cinder."

"This wizard must be special if you are willing to seek him out."

"He's one that I can tolerate," she said.

"And where will we find this wizard?"

"Oldham."

"Perfect... it's on the way." Grey Cloak scanned the faces, man and dragon. All eyes were on him, and the time had come for him to make important decisions. "This is who is going. Anya and Cinder. Streak and I. Dyphestive, we aren't taking Rock. Is there another dragon you'd prefer to ride?"

"Any volunteers?" Dyphestive asked.

The pack of middling dragons came to life and said, "Oh, me, me, me!" They jumped on one another, spread their wings, and posed.

"I'm the fastest," Feather said.

"No, I am!" Slick replied as he slipped in front of her.

Slicer jumped in front of Dyphestive and bared his long claws. "Take me! I'm deadly!"

Even Chubby wandered over and said in his dull voice, "I'd like to go."

With the dragons crowding him, Dyphestive said, "I'm flattered, but I don't see a fair way to do this. I'll tell you what. We'll draw stems. Do you know what that is?"

The dragons shook their heads.

Dyphestive hurried out of the cave, gathered some stems that grew out of the ground, and broke one so that it was half the size of the others. He filled his hand with them and returned to the Vault. "It's very easy. Whoever draws the short stem goes."

One by one, each dragon grabbed a stem with their front paw. Together, they compared them.

Slicer held the short stem. "I won! I won!"

"Aaah," the other dragons moaned as they wandered away with their long necks down.

Slicer draped his tail over Dyphestive's shoulder. "Don't worry about those losers. You have me now. The deadliest," he said in his velvety voice and gnashed his teeth. "I can't wait to kill something."

Feather was the last one to walk by Dyphestive, and she said, "You should have picked me."

"Sorry," Dyphestive said. He reached out to touch her tail, but she slunk away.

"That settles it, except for one more addition. We are going to need a mule," Grey Cloak said.

"A mule?" Anya asked.

"That's right. We aren't going to travel light. We'll need to be prepared with plenty of equipment and weapons. And I'll need a dragon that is strong and fast to carry the extra load. What do you say, Feather? Are you up for it?"

Feather stopped in her tracks then rose and spread her wings as proudly as a peacock. Her pretty pink eyes shone like stars when she said, "Am I ever!"

Grey Cloak turned toward the bowels of the Vault and said, "Gear up, everyone. We have a long flight ahead."

13

HIGH ROCK

ZORA, Gorva, and Razor were flying southwest with the sky gnomes on the backs of giant vultures. It was an overcast day, with the sun hiding behind the sheets of clouds that hovered high overhead. On the orders of Jumax, the leader of the Southern Storm, they were being taken on a mission to the Cliffs of the Beast.

"How much longer?" Zora shouted into Durmost's ear.

The gnome shrugged and said, "It won't be long. The cliffs are near, but we can't get close. The Scales are our sworn enemy. If we cross into their territory, they're certain to attack, and the mission will be doomed." He motioned ahead. "Can you see that far-away formation of rocks? You will go there."

Razor rode in a vulture's saddle behind another sky

gnome. They were flying beside Zora and Durmost. "*What is he saying?*" he shouted at Zora.

She pointed at the rock formation. "We're almost there!"

Razor nodded. "Good, because this vulture stinks." He caught the gnome looking back at him and said, "It's either him or you. I think you both need a bird bath."

Durmost made a hand signal and led his vulture to the ground, and the others followed them to the dusty earth.

"We will wait for you," Durmost said.

Zora climbed out of her vulture's saddle and hopped to the ground. "Those cliffs are at least a league of walking. They will see us coming."

"No, the Scales sleep in the day and hunt at night. You must find the Ear of the Gods, a golden relic of our people. It is in their lair, and you might need to slay the beast to do so."

Razor and Gorva joined Zora. All of them were decked out with their full array of weaponry. Gorva carried a spear with a wicked-looking razor-sharp head that Jumax had given her.

"What sort of beast are we talking about?" Razor asked.

Durmost shrugged.

"How helpful," Razor said with a shake of his head. "And why haven't you taken the ear for yourself? Why do we need to do it?"

"The Scales will see our kind coming. They won't be concerned with the likes of you," Durmost said.

"I thought you said they slept in the day," Gorva said.

"They do. Well, most of them. Their bats sleep, as do the lizard men, but they do post sentries," the sky gnome replied.

The three of them exchanged concerned looks.

"What sort of sentries are you talking about?" Gorva asked.

"Avoid the wildlife. The shrieking cacti. The needle blossoms cry out a warning." Durmost tapped his skull and winked. "If you avoid them, your mission will be simple. Don't get too close."

"I don't like the sound of this," Razor said. "I say we move out on our own."

"You owe a life debt. Repay it by fulfilling this quest, or your life will be taken," Durmost reminded them. He offered his final words of wisdom. "Follow the smell to where the beast dwells."

"Whatever happened to the days when you helped people without expecting payment?" Razor turned toward the distant cliffs and walked away.

Zora nodded at Gorva. "Let's go."

"Don't take long. They wake at dusk, and the lair comes alive with them. They fill the skies and hunt the night. Remember, the prayers of the Southern Storm are with you!" Durmost stated.

They hadn't walked a third of a league before Razor said, "My boots are burning. Bloody desert is as hot as fire."

Zora nodded. The southern climate was as hot as it was barren, and she'd sweated through her clothing already. "On the bright side, it will probably be pretty cool inside those caves."

"If we make it inside. I feel like lizard men are going to pour out of those caves at any moment," Razor replied. "Bizarre. This entire quest is bizarre."

"I agree," Gorva said.

"Now I know I must be dreaming."

They hurried across the broken landscape of rocks and desert bushes. Razor led them clear of cacti and needle bushes. The trek to the Cliffs of the Beast left them all soaking in sweat by the time they arrived at his jagged base. The cliffs had a steep slant with rocky hand- and footholds leading up to the cave entrances.

"A nasty climb. Great," Razor said as he wiped his face with a cloth. "I hate climbing."

"I'll go," Zora said. She toyed with the Scarf of Shadows, which hung around her neck. "Perhaps it will be simple if they can't see me."

"We need to stay together. Besides, you don't even know where to start looking. There is no telling what is inside that lair." Gorva grabbed Zora by the arm. "You'll need protection."

Zora spied the nearest cave from the ground. It had a

small ledge at the entrance and was a thirty-foot climb. "I'm going in there. You can wait for me there, and well, I'll scream if I need you." She adjusted Crane's satchel and scurried up the rocks. Her nimble fingers found purchase, and she scaled the rocks like a squirrel. She waved at her friends, lifted the scarf over her nose, and vanished.

Razor stared at the cave Zora had entered and commented, "She's a brave little thing. I wish I could climb like that."

"Maybe you can't, but I can." She handed him her spear. "Toss this up to me, and I'll lower a rope down to you."

"Sounds like a plan." He watched Gorva climb the rocks with the ease of a mountain goat and said, "Nice view."

Gorva shook her head. She entered the mouth of the cave and beckoned for her spear.

"I'm not very good at throwing things either," Razor admitted. He flung it upward by the bottom of the shaft and watched Gorva catch it with ease. "Nice catch."

Gorva uncoiled a rope and lowered it down to Razor's position. "Come up. Hurry."

Razor locked his fingers around the rope, set his boots against the rock, and started the climb. "This isn't so bad."

Gorva let the rope slip when he was halfway up.

"Goy! Don't do that!"

"What's the matter? Are you afraid I'll let you fall?"

He continued the climb hand over hand. "Well, I wouldn't blame you if you did, with how ornery I am." With a grunt, he climbed into the mouth of the cave. "Say, where's Zora?"

14

IT TOOK a few moments for Zora to catch her breath and let her eyes adjust to the darkness. Her heart beat like a jackrabbit's as she crept deeper into the cave and covered her nose.

Whew, this place smells awful! Like a dirty animal cage.

On cat's feet, she wandered farther into the lair. Her keen eyes adjusted to the outline of the tunnel. Twenty-five yards inside, the crude lines of the natural cave turned into tunnels that had been carved out with chisels and hammers. The walls were solid rock, and an eerie light was at the end of the tunnel.

With one hand on the handle of her dagger, she made her way to the end of the tunnel and came upon an intersection with three more tunnels. A large black boulder sat in the middle of the intersection with images of lizard men riding bats carved all over it. A patch of glowing quartz was in the roof of the high chamber. The shiny minerals could be seen glowing down inside the other tunnels.

She glanced up and noticed more tunnels behind the ledges above her that created several levels.

Dirty acorns. This place is a labyrinth. What has Jumax gotten us into?

Zora closed her eyes and used her hearing, hoping to make out the sound of something living. The only thing she heard was the sound of her heartbeat.

Dragon dung. Well, I have to start somewhere. Here goes.

Mindful to remember where she'd entered, she moved into the adjacent tunnel. The stone floor curved upward in a steep climb, and she quickly found herself standing on the ledge of the next level, looking down on the spot where she'd entered.

I don't think this is progress.

She clasped the collar of her shirt and fanned herself. She'd shed a lot of weight, and her previously tight clothes didn't cling to her body anymore. She was back in shape, as any good thief would be.

She went back down to the level where she'd started and entered another tunnel that wound downward. The farther she walked, the fouler the stench became. She pinched the Scarf of Shadows over her nose.

This is awful. Follow the stench and find the beast.

The tunnel became one long downward spiral, and when it flattened out, she was standing in a huge underground chamber with a high ceiling supported by huge stone pillars carved out of rock. Her jaw tightened, as did her grip on her dagger. Scores of lizard men were curled up on the floor with their tails wrapped around their bodies like blankets.

Sweet dragons!

Zora backed up. Her foot bumped against a small brass bowl on the floor. The metal scraped over the floor, but to her, it sounded like a cymbal.

A lizard man raised his head. His yellow eyes looked toward the entrance, and his thin black tongue flicked out of his mouth. Slowly, he turned his scaly head from side to side, scanning the room like a hungry predator.

Without moving a muscle, Zora remained in her position. Instinctively, she looked down at her hands and saw nothing.

Whew!

The Scarf of Shadows worked in tandem with subtlety. Its mystical powers would diminish in a sudden act such as an attack.

Slowly, the lizard man lay his head back down to rest. At the same time, he grabbed his spear and pulled it closer to his chest. His eyes remained open, staring blankly at Zora for the longest time.

Don't look at him. Don't look at him.

Zora tore her gaze away from the lizard man and focused on the others in the chamber. The lizard men slept with their weapons close by. Spears, crude swords, and hatchets lay near them. Most of the lizard men were bare-chested and armored naturally with corded muscle bulging under their rough snakelike skin. They wore furs and leather. Many of them had jewelry on their necks and wrists made from bones and natural stones. Not a single one of them made a sound. They lay still, as if they weren't breathing, hibernating.

A primitive bunch. That should work in my favor. I mean, how smart can you be when you clearly never bathe?

The only other exit was one across the room. It was a great opening to what appeared to be a sunken chamber that showed the warm glow of a fire.

She glanced at the lizard man that had been staring her way before. His eyes had closed. Watching her step, she began picking her way across the floor. Moving on the balls of her feet, she took her time, careful not to brush against any of them. When she was halfway across the room, a rustle from above caught her ear. She lifted her eyes and stared into the black ceiling. The ceiling moved.

Her veins turned to ice as she stared upward in stark horror.

Huge bats, larger than men, hung from the ceiling of the cave. Their leathery wings were wrapped around their bodies as tight as leather. Their ugly faces were an image of horror. Dozens of sets of eyes stared down at her with a penetrating gaze. She lifted a trembling hand, as if to wave, and watched their eyes follow.

No, they can't be watching me. Bats are blind, aren't they?

15

SHRINKING underneath the gaze of the bats, Zora slowly backed away. She stepped on a spear, which rolled under her foot, and she fell over a lizard man.

The lizard man sat upright and blinked. His thin black tongue flicked out of his mouth as he looked about. He looked straight through Zora, who sat only inches away from his face. She didn't breathe.

With a grunt, the lizard man kicked one of his comrades in the leg, lay down, and closed his eyes.

Zora let out a silent breath and resumed a slower, more careful trek across the chamber. She glanced upward at the bats, but their eyes were closed or averted. She stepped over the last lizard man in her path and made her way to the opening of the next chamber.

Her nose crinkled, and her eyes watered. *This is awful.*

She went down into the sunken chamber, which was a large cave. Torches were bracketed to the walls, lit by hunks of quartz that burned like fire. A large golden object on the far side of the room caught her eye. It was as big as a man's head and crudely shaped like a man's ear. It glinted with the vibrant colors of many gemstones. It could only be one thing.

The Ear of the Gods!

Zora scanned the cave from top to bottom. The floor and ceiling were natural with crude rock formations, and she saw no sign of a living beast, but the foul smell of excrement suggested otherwise.

She crept deeper into the dank dwelling and navigated toward the alcove. The floor was slimy in places. She slid but caught her balance on a cluster of rocks that was covered in a strange green goo.

Yuck! I don't even want to know what this is.

She wiped her hand on her trousers and continued.

The Ear of the Gods was displayed in full view inside a nook within the alcove. The only other things inside the nook were some small cacti-like plants growing along the base of the wall.

Zora ran her keen gaze over the alcove. She didn't see any pressure plates in the floor, slits, or triggers along the walls. The dwelling place of the artifact was as solid as the day it had been created.

She entered the alcove and baby-stepped toward the

hunk of gold. She stood before it with her eyes wide. There were more gems than she could count. The precious stones adorned the gold like holes in a sponge.

This thing must be worth a kingdom.

She blew into her hands and wiggled her fingers. *Here goes.*

After muttering a quick prayer, she reached out and picked up the Ear of the Gods. Her spine tingled the moment she grabbed it.

It's heavy.

She wasn't entirely sure how the Scarf of Shadows worked, but she remained invisible, while the gold remained in full view.

It's not ideal, but I should be able to steal my way out of here while they're still sleeping.

With a spin on her heel, she turned back toward the way she'd come.

A subtle sound caught her attention. She looked behind her. The skin from the small cacti plants began to peel away. Pink cords, like tongues, rose from inside of the little plants and let out an awful shrieking sound that could wake the dead. *Skreee!*

Zora's knees buckled. She swayed and fell into the alcove's wall. Her stomach turned, and her strength was sapped from her limbs. She fought to hold on to the Ear of the Gods, but it slipped from her fingers.

No. Don't lose it. No.

"She's been down in there awhile, hasn't she?" Razor asked. He was doing tricks with one of his daggers, flipping it around in a showy fashion like a magician. "So where did you learn to fight so well?"

"I don't think we should be talking," Gorva responded quietly. They were still waiting inside the entrance of the cave, and she'd ventured a few yards in. She cupped her ear. "Keep silent. I think I hear something."

"It's probably your heartbeat. It can be really loud when you're excited. A lot of women say that when they're around me." He flipped his dagger hand over hand and slipped it back into his sheath. "So, tell me... you're a natural. Or a daughter of a natural. And your father, Hogrim, taught you to fight, right?"

Gorva gave him a disappointed look. "You have difficulty remaining silent, don't you?"

He shrugged. "What can I say? I'm a master conversationalist. Every bit as good with my lips as I am with my sword."

"You must be very proud. But a true master of conversation would be able to master nonconversation as well," she said.

Razor snaked out another dagger and tapped it on the palm of his free hand. "You know what I think? I think you are a pint-half-empty sort of person. I'm a pint-half-full sort."

"Your skull is half full."

Razor smiled. "That's a good one. You see, you can be a joy when you want to. As a matter of fact, how about you change your name to Joy. It's more welcoming than Gorva. I know that screams orcen, but with your beauty, I think Joy would be a better fit. I have an aunt and uncle back home, Earl and Joy. There's no finer a couple. You should meet them."

She glowered at him. "If you ever call me Joy, I'll kill you."

Razor raised an eyebrow and said, "Hmmm... how about Francis?"

A terrifying sound came screaming through the tunnel and hit them like a tidal wave and knocked them both backward.

Skreee!

Razor fell to one knee and covered his ears, shouting, "*What is that sound?*"

Gorva yelled back, "*Trouble! Come on!*"

16

THE SHRIEKING STOPPED. At least, Zora thought it stopped, but her ears were still ringing. Dizzy, she lifted her head. A horde of lizard men, weapons in hand, had her surrounded.

Bloody biscuits. I'm a dead half elf now.

To her surprise, she still cradled the Ear of the Gods in her invisible hands. *Unless...*

Taking full advantage of her invisibility, she lifted the golden ear from the ground and started to rise.

The lizard men gave alarmed hisses and backed away. Their slanted eyes widened, and they clung to their bone necklaces.

"It is a sign!" one of the lizard men stated. He had a broad build and a bulging girth. He carried a spear with bones and feathers adorning the shaft, and he shook it like a rattle. "A sign we must follow!"

Zora's eyes widened. *I can work with this.*

She lifted the Ear of the Gods higher and marched quietly out of the alcove. The lizard men parted, their gazes fixed on the golden ear. She took one last look behind her. The small screeching cacti had collapsed and hung limp over the wall of the cave.

Thank goodness that's over.

With the lizard men clearing a path, she made it halfway across the chamber and started her ascent into the large chamber outside.

A second lizard man, dressed like a shaman in small bones, hide, and feathers, barred her path. He wore a crown made from antlers and carried a large cudgel. His tail swished over the floor behind him, and he said, "Stop!"

Zora hesitated and held her spot on the steps.

I shouldn't have done that.

"It is a sign," the first lizard man with the spear said. "We must follow it, High Shaman! It is a sign!"

The high shaman's eyes narrowed on the Ear of the Gods. "No! I sense treachery." He drew in a deep breath through the small black nostrils of his snout. "I smell deceit. There is warm-blooded flesh afoot. That is why the alarm sounded!"

Great. They all had to be stupid except for one.

She resumed her march up the steps. As she did so, she

moved the golden ear back and forth in the shape of a smile.

The high shaman shuffled backward, but he drew his club over his broad shoulders.

Uh-oh, he's going to swing.

The chamber beyond the high shaman was clear, but his serpentine eyes bore into her. With the object suspended above her head, she moved left. The high shaman moved in the way. She went right, and he shuffled into her path.

Horseshoes!

In the wink of an eye, the high shaman's tail whipped Zora's legs out from under her. She landed hard on her backside. The Scarf of Shadows slipped, and she became visible again.

The high shaman thrust his finger at her and said, "See? Defiler!"

The horde of lizard men's voices erupted in shocked and angry hisses.

"If you so much as lay a claw on me, I'll destroy the Ear of the Gods with my magical powers!" she shouted.

The high shaman withdrew his fist and gave her an uncertain look.

She rose back to her feet and held the golden ear high. "That's right! One magic word from me, and *boom*!"

"You have no such power," the high shaman said. "You are no more than a thief!"

"Is that so? Then smell this!"

She stuck her fist out and waved the Ring of Mist under his nose. The metal petals opened, and a fine mist sprayed the mouth of the high shaman. His eyes rolled up inside his head, and he crumpled to the floor.

Zora turned and faced the horde of lizard men crammed inside the smaller chamber. She gave them a long wave goodbye and said, "So long, you slithering donkey skulls."

Then she pivoted on one foot and ran.

Razor and Gorva navigated the tunnels shoulder to shoulder. Two short swords filled his grip. They were better for close-quarters fighting. The ear-splitting screeching had come to a halt, and the caves instantly quieted.

With his skin crawling, Razor said, "Are you sure you don't want a shorter weapon? You can't fight with that big stick in these tunnels."

"I'll do fine. And you should hush. I'm trying to listen," Gorva replied. "You need to pay attention so that we don't become lost."

"Don't worry. I never get lost."

They exited the tunnel into a chamber with several levels going up to more tunnels.

Gorva's nose crinkled. "She must have come this way."

"You can smell her?"

"No, but I can smell something awful. Find the smell, and find where the beast dwells. That's what the gnome said."

Razor scratched his head with the pommel of his sword. "Is that what he said? Or was it *Avoid the smell where the monster dwells*, because I don't like the way this place is stinking."

She moved toward the adjacent tunnel. "When I find the time, I'm going to sew your lips shut."

"Why would you want to ruin a pair of lips as soft as these?" He puckered up and kissed the air. "Your heart would be filled with regret."

Gorva sighed and entered the next tunnel.

Razor followed.

When she stopped, he started to speak, and she sealed his lips shut with her fingers and pushed him back out of the tunnel.

Zora ran by on one of the higher levels. She carried a gold rock and vanished into the tunnels.

"Did you see that?" Gorva asked.

Razor nodded. The next thing he knew, Zora emerged from the tunnel, running.

"What's going on?" Gorva asked

"No time to talk." Zora sped right by them. "Run!"

17

Zora raced through the tunnel and came upon a pair of lizard men carrying clubs. The slithering brutes blocked the passage and came at her.

The first lizard man, a long-necked fiend, swung at her head with a two-handed club.

With the Ear of the Gods cradled in her hand, she ducked the club, did a backspin in the opposite direction, and slipped around the lizard man's back. She found herself waiting underneath a two-handed club held by a second neckless lizard man bulging with muscle. Saliva dripped from his yellow teeth, and he brought the club down.

Zora hopped to the side. The club cracked into the stone floor.

She dashed away and took a glance over her shoulder.

The lizard men turned in pursuit and let out angry shouts. "Come back, warm blood!"

Gorva and Razor came around the bend in the tunnel and plowed through the lizard men like they were scarecrows in a corn field. The lizard men's snouts bashed into the floor, and Gorva and Razor trampled them.

"Lead the way, little woman," Razor said. "Because more are coming!"

The lizard men lying on the floor started to rise, but the horde ran right over them.

"Zora, keep running. No matter what you do, keep running!" Razor said as he chased after her and Gorva. "I'll hold them off. You run for the sky gnomes. 'Cause there is no turning back now!"

She paused inside the tunnel where they'd entered. "No, we all need to run! Together!"

"They'll slaughter us in the open field! Go! Both of you!" he said with a nod. "I can fight them off!"

"That's crazy!" Zora said. "They'll butcher you!"

"Thanks for the vote of confidence!" Razor shoved her and Gorva down the tunnel. "But we don't have much of a choice, do we?"

"He's right," Gorva said. "We must go!"

She gave Razor one last fleeting look and said, "You're too brave for your own good."

He nodded. "I know. Now, scoot!"

Razor spun the handles of his short swords over his wrists then tightened his grip and muttered, "I can't believe she said I'd get butchered. Does she even know what a blade master is?" He took a deep breath. "It's time to take it personally and get out of this snake pit alive."

The first wave of lizard men came. They were paired up and crammed into the tunnel as far as Razor could see. They carried swords, knives, and hatchets. Their bone jewelry rattled as they ran toward him and hissed.

"Come on! I could use a new pair of lizard-skin boots!" Razor said as he crouched into a battle stance with his swords cocked back at his sides.

The lizard men came at him in a rush. Razor lunged forward and thrust both swords into the bellies of the lizard men in the wink of an eye. He didn't stop there. Before the first pair fell, he squirted between them and chopped the next closest lizard man down with a strike to the neck.

His dripping blades carved through the lizard men's defenses and had them scrambling for their lives. Anything that moved Razor stabbed. Their dark blood leaked onto the floor, and they hissed in pain.

The onslaught became a slaughter. Razor's blood continued to boil as the charge of battle coursed through him. Gone was the charming visage of a spirited young man. It was replaced by the mask of a stone-cold killer.

"Reap the whirlwind!" he shouted.

Slice! Chop! Hack! Steel ripped through scales and severed bones. Fingers and hands were lost. Bleeding, the lizard men fled. Their senses had been dulled by their hibernation, and Razor made them pay for it.

A fleeing lizard man dared a look over his shoulder. Razor took his head off with a single swing. He forced them deeper into the caves, where they were bred in the bowels of the earth. He forced them to hide in their own home, battling them back to the intersection he'd passed through before. They vanished into the tunnels like rats.

"Come back and fight, you forked-tongue cowards!" He beat his blood-splattered chest. "Face the Razor!"

Razor stood in the intersection with his swords down at his sides, dark blood dripping from the blades. He scanned the tunnel entrances high and low. With the bloodlust still upon him, he asked, "What's the matter? Scared of dying? You don't like the taste of steel? The sting of death?" His chest heaved. "I don't blame you. I'd be scared, too, if I had to face me!"

A strange sound emerged from the depths of the tunnels. It was a loud hollow sound, like a deep humming that grew in strength and volume. The cave floor trembled.

"Kiss my steel," he muttered. His blood cooled, and he started back down the tunnel from whence he'd come.

A high-pitched shriek blasted out of the tunnels above him. A giant bat flew out of one tunnel, jettisoned over the gap, and squeezed into the next tunnel. The other tunnels spewed out massive bats.

"Lizard men are one thing. Giant bats are another." He turned and ran down the tunnel. "Run, man. Run. The flying rats are coming!"

A giant bat screeched. Razor looked behind him. The nasty monster was squeezing its body through the tunnel and coming right at him with alarming speed. He increased his speed. His wounded leg burned like fire. A crack of daylight caught his eye. The cave opened at the end of the tunnel, offering escape. He sped toward the bright and open sky. The giant bat closed the distance.

Razor jumped out into the daylight and crawled along the ledge of the Cliffs of the Beast. The bat burst out of the cave with a lizard man on its back. It scurried toward Razor and latched its clawed feet on his ankle, beat its wings, and leaped into the air.

The next thing Razor knew, he was hanging upside down and flying through the air. He screamed, "Zooora!"

18

ZORA STOOD on the ledge of the caves and stared down the short climb then tossed the Ear of the Gods to the ground and scrambled down the rocks. She jumped down the last ten feet, scooped up the golden ear, and started running. Gorva matched her stride for stride.

"We shouldn't have left Razor," Zora said with a tear coming down from the corner of her eye. "We shouldn't have!"

Gorva grabbed her arm and said, "Don't stop! Don't look back! You must run like a devil!" She slapped Zora on the behind. "Now, go! I'll go back for Razor!"

"But—"

"Go!" Gorva gave her a hard shove in the back.

Zora continued running across the dusty field. The

sandy ground spat up behind her boots, and she left a trail in the dust.

This is madness! They are going to get killed! And it's my fault!

A quick look over her shoulder revealed Gorva's long legs closing the distance between her and the cliffs. She arrived at the base, grabbed the rocks, and started to climb.

She's crazy. They are both out of their skulls!

Zora swung her gaze forward and almost ran into a cactus. She sprang to the side like a deer, but the damage was done. The strange cactus plant started to peel open like a banana. A fleshy tongue inside began to shudder, and it let out an ear-splitting howl. *Skreee!*

The jarring sound forced Zora to her knees. She dropped the artifact and covered her ears. In all directions, the screeching cacti came to life in a chorus filled with the destructive sound.

Zora curled up like a baby, with her fingers plugging her ears. She rocked back and forth on the ground.

I can't do this. I can't do this.

Waves of nausea crashed inside her belly. Bright white spots appeared behind her closed eyes.

No. I have to fight. I can't let them down.

She forced her eyelids open, unplugged her ears, and grabbed the Ear of the Gods.

Skreee!

On legs like noodles, she staggered forward, searching

for the right direction to go. She shuffled left and right and came face-to-face with a spiny-needle tree. Its branches were like bones that were covered in needles as fine as cat hairs.

Not that way.

The tree pulsed and flexed. Needles shot out of its ghost-white bark and showered Zora's clothing and skin.

"Auugh!" She ran forward. Her face and arms broke out in tiny red blisters. "It burns!"

Somehow, she kept going, fighting her way through the maddening environment determined to consume her. She put one foot in front of the other and screamed back at the wild, "Shut your mouths!"

Skreee!

She hadn't made it two hundred yards before she lost her footing and crashed down into a dry gulch. Her head smacked against a rock. Blood ran into her eyes when she looked up into the open sky.

Skreee!

The gulch shielded her from part of the overbearing torrent of sound. She caught her breath and pulled needles from her face. The blisters on her arms were a sight to see, and her stomach turned again. She forced herself back up.

I should never have left Raven Cliff.

She lifted the Scarf of Shadows over her nose. Its powers were lost for the day, and she didn't vanish. All she could do was run and hope that her enemy couldn't catch her. She took a peek out of the gulch. Giant bats with green-brown lizard men on their backs were flying out of the cave. Escape would be easier said than done. *Dirty acorns. I knew I should never have joined Talon.*

"Let go of me!" Razor shouted. He stared upward at the hairy gray belly of the giant bat lifting him higher into the sky. Hanging upside down, he watched the ground below him race by. "On second thought, don't drop me yet."

The lizard-man rider leaned over the side of the bat and looked down at him. His tongue flicked out of his mouth, and he said, "It's going to be a long fall, human! But I'll find you a comfortable bed of rocks for you to die in."

"Thanks for the offer, but I don't plan on dying today, Snake Face!" He let go of both of his swords and let them fall to the ground.

He and the lizard man couldn't have been any higher than one hundred feet in the air, and the giant bats' wings labored to lift them higher.

The lizard man smacked the bat with a lash and shouted, "Upward! Upward!"

Razor chuckled. He was loaded down with weapons and gear, and his body was hard bone and muscle. The bat was only accustomed to one rider and smaller prey, like a sky gnome, it seemed.

He did a sit-up in midair and grabbed the harness that made up the bat's skimpy saddle with one hand.

"What are you *doing*?" the lizard man shouted. He leaned over his saddle again and started stabbing at Razor with a javelin. "Let go, you fool!"

Razor grabbed the javelin with his free hand and yanked it away. "It seems to me that if this bat goes down, we both go down!" He stared into the lizard man's eyes and pointed the javelin at the giant bat's bowels. "Are you ready to die with me?"

"We don't fear death!"

"Great. Then we have something in common. Neither do I!" Razor rammed the javelin deep into the belly of the bat.

The winged monster bucked.

"No!" the lizard man shouted. "You fool! You'll kill us both!"

"That's the idea!" He stabbed the bat once more. Nasty, murky fluids spilled out onto his face. "Yuck! Now hurry up and land this thing!"

The bat's wings folded like a tent. It plummeted toward the earth. Watching the world rush up to greet them, Razor and the lizard man both screamed.

19

THE LIZARD MEN emerged from the caves and fastened their gazes on Gorva, who ascended the hill. "Kill her! Kill her!" they shouted.

Clinging to the rocks with one hand, Gorva shoved her spear into a lizard man standing on the ledge and flung him down. He plummeted headfirst, and his bones cracked when he hit the bottom.

On a higher level of the caves, a lizard man shaman decorated in a headdress of feathers and bones pointed down at her with a large cudgel and said, "Slay her! Slay the orc woman!"

Gorva speared the leg of a second lizard man and swiped the legs out from under a third. Both of them tumbled down the steep, rocky hillside.

"Nooo!" the high shaman yelled. "She is only one! We are many! Swarm her!"

Taking advantage of the gap between the wave of attacks, Gorva scurried up to the next ledge. She saw no sign of Razor, but giant bats began to emerge from the mouths of the caves with lizard men riding on their backs. She heard a desperate shout and turned her head around. A huge bat had Razor caught in its talons and was flying away from the cliffs.

She cocked her spear back over her shoulder, but the bat was too far away. "At least he's alive."

"What are you waiting for, brethren? Slay the orc!" the high shaman yelled again. A bat crawled out from one of the cave mouths, and the high shaman climbed onto its back. "I will retrieve the Ear of the Gods. When I return, the orc had better be dead!" The bat spread its wings and took flight.

Gorva stood on the ledge with her back to the hill. She adjusted her footing.

Lizard men approached her from both sides of the same ledge and penned her in. On the ledge above, they started hurling small rocks at her.

A rock bashed her in the shoulder. "Cowards!"

A lizard man carrying a long sword approached from the right and lunged. She poked him in the chest with her longer weapon and pushed him off the ledge. A second lizard man hurried in from the left with an ax raised high.

She rammed him in the gut using the butt end of her spear. He doubled over and fell.

"I can do this all day," she said as she thwarted one attack after another while getting pummeled in the head and shoulders with rocks. Between her attacks, she caught one stone and flung it back into the face of the lizard man that had thrown it. The rock hit him hard in the snout. He fell and bounced off of the ledge, and she stabbed him on the way down to the bottom of the cliffs.

Dozens of bats flew over the plains, and the cacti plants screamed in the fields. Scores of lizard men crept along the ledges toward her, while others climbed down to the dusty field and raced across it in a search for the Ear of the Gods.

Gorva killed every lizard man that came in her path.

"She is strong!" one of them shouted from above. "She's no ordinary orc! Use the nets!"

Two lizard men appeared on the ledge from two levels above and hurried to a position above Gorva.

"I don't do nets." She gutted a lizard man on the right with her spear and shoved him backward into another as the net was hurled down at her.

A pair of lizard men charging her from the left were caught in the net. It carried them over the edge, and their bodies crashed to the rocky ground.

Catching sight of more lizard men with nets coming, Gorva hurled her spear into a lizard man that had survived his fall and hit him in the chest. She hopped off the ledge and slid down the cliffside. She launched herself off of the rocks the last twelve feet and landed on another lizard man who was pushing up on his hands and knees. His body collapsed under her weight, and his ribs cracked under her feet.

She fetched her spear out of the other lizard man's body and said, "Thanks for holding this," and took off running with more than a score of lizard men running right behind her.

Razor watched in wide-eyed horror as he plummeted toward the broken plains, waiting for the kiss of death. "Aaauuuwwww!"

The giant bat he'd gored spasmed. Its collapsed wings spread open, catching the wind, and it lifted for a moment. The fall slowed, turning into a fast glide with the rugged plains racing below Razor's boots. He plowed through a screaming cactus or two, and the giant bat crashed face first to the ground and rolled like a tumbleweed.

Razor ended up planted inside a small bed of cacti that had bright-orange blossoms. He was stuck in the thorns, and his bones ached all over. "Oh, great."

He pulled his arm out of the ugly thorns, drew a long sword, and used it like a cane. He pushed out of the prickly bush. "Ugh!" His bare arms and backside were covered in thorns. "I hope these things aren't poisonous." But he could barely hear himself speak for all of the shrieking plants.

The giant bat lay on the ground nearby. Its wings twitched, and its body spasmed. The lizard man staggered across the ground on two feet, holding his bleeding head and shaking it. He caught sight of Razor and screamed, "You killed my bat! You killed my bat!" He charged with his bare claws extended.

Razor slew him with a single stroke and said, "And I killed you, too, lizard man."

The shrieking plants silenced. The shadows of bats passed overhead. A roar of voices came from the plains.

Lizard men were running toward Razor with blood in their eyes and a trail of dust behind them.

He plucked some thorns from his butt and said, "This is going to get ugly."

20

ZORA LUMBERED through the gulch with the deadweight of the Ear of the Gods in her arms. The hunk of gold weighed several pounds, and her arms and back were burning. The needles in her arm didn't help either. Her skin burned as she pushed her way through the channel, which went in the opposite direction of the cliffs.

Taking a quick glance upward, she noticed a pair of bats and their riders soaring her way. She crouched in the gulch and hid her body in the rocks while using the shadows to conceal her.

The bats let out eerie sonar calls that carried through the gulch in a wave of awful sound. Zora curled up in a ball.

The bats and their shadows passed.

Whew! Does everything in this dragon-forsaken stretch have to make the most awful sounds?

All of a sudden, the shrieking cacti quieted, and she could hear herself think.

Lords of the Air, I hope that is over.

She set down the golden ear and climbed up the wall of the long ravine. Lizard men traveled in small packs, many of which were aiming for the ravine. No more than fifty yards away, one of the packs jumped into the gulch and appeared to be heading her way.

Ettin's ears!

The bats soared above in small swooping circles. The high shaman of the lizard men was one of the ones that she could see. He flew on the largest bat, and he shouted at the top of his lungs, "Find the infidels! Find the ear!"

She saw no sign of Razor or Gorva, and her stomach sank.

Don't even think it, Zora. She wiped a long strand of sweaty hair from her eye. *They're alive. They must be!*

She slid back into the gulch, picked up the ear, and started running again.

How'd I get into this mess? Jumax. He's handsome, but he's mad, I believe. A life debt. Insanity.

The gulch took a sudden elbow turn. She made haste around the bend and ran into the back of Gorva.

Gorva grabbed her by the collar and slammed her hard into the ravine floor. Her nostrils flared, and she was lathered in sweat like a racing horse. "Zora!" She hauled her back to her feet. "Apologies. I thought you were a lizard."

"Do I look that bad?"

Gorva gave her a brisk hug. "Of course not, sister!"

"They're flooding the gulch. We'd better keep moving." She offered the ear to Gorva. "Will you carry this? I hate to sound like a weakling, but I'm spent."

Gorva stuck the artifact in the crook of her elbow like a loaf of bread. "Not a problem." She tapped the butt of her spear on the ground. "Let's go."

Trailing after Gorva, Zora said, "Did you see Razor?"

"A bat caught him, but he was still alive the last that I saw."

"How'd you escape?"

"I'm very fast, and they broke off pursuit, I believe to focus on finding the Ear of Corn."

"You mean the Ear of the Gods."

Gorva looked back at her and cracked a smile that bared her canines. "Sorry, I must be getting hungry."

The deep gulch began to ascend toward the surface.

"We are running out of ravine," Gorva said as she came to a stop.

Both of them flattened inside the ravine as more bats soared overhead.

"They are widening their search patterns," Gorva said with sweat dripping from her chin. "And there is nowhere to search but here."

"Get away from me, Bat Face!" a man outside of the gulch hollered.

Zora and Gorva scrambled to the top of the gulch.

Razor stood on the ground, locked in battle with three giant bats and their riders. He was in the middle, fending them off with the strokes of two blades.

Gorva stuffed the golden ear toward Zora's belly. "It's your turn to hold this."

Before Zora could get a word out of her mouth, Gorva was off and running toward the bats. She snuck in behind a bat and rider, took a flying leap, landed between the bat's wings, pinned the lizard man to the saddle, and sank the spear through the bat's back until it popped out of its sternum.

"Grisly," Zora muttered as she watched Gorva rip the spear back out.

Razor spun his blades around his body in a lethal whirlwind of steel and cut open the face of a giant bat then brought down an overhead chop that split open its skull.

A frenzied lizard man leaped from the dying bat's saddle and hurled a set of bolos that wrapped around Razor's neck and clocked him in the head. He stumbled to a knee as another giant bat landed near him with its jaws open to bite.

Zora sprang out of her hiding spot, leaving the golden ear behind, and charged blindly into the fray.

Gorva fought off another giant bat with her spear. She poked at its face and belly, keeping the monster at bay.

Zora filled her hands with steel daggers and jammed them underneath the wing of the giant bat attacking Razor. She pushed the points in deep. The bat shrieked like a banshee. Its flapping wings knocked her to the ground.

"You're a brave one. I'll give you that!" Razor said as he hooked his arms under hers and dragged her away from danger. The bolos hung over his shoulders like a necklace. He had thorns in his bloody face. "Stay close."

Gorva joined them in the center of a growing wave of landing bats and swarming lizard men. The enemy had them surrounded, and they had nowhere to go.

Razor spat blood on the ground, wrist-spun his blades, and said, "Which one of you uglies is going to die first?"

21

———————

Surrounded by more of the enemy than they could count, Zora, Gorva, and Razor watched the high shaman descend from the heights and land among his brethren.

From his perch on the bat's saddle, he narrowed his eyes at them and said, "I am Igmonbald, high shaman of this clan. You will tell me where the Ear of the Gods is."

With a shrug, Zora replied, "What Ear of the Gods? I didn't see any Ear of the Gods." She looked at Gorva and Razor. "Did you see an Ear of the Gods?"

"No, but I could eat a giant ear of corn. I'm famished," Gorva replied.

Razor cupped his ear and leaned in the high shaman's direction. "Did you say you can't *hear the gods*? I can't hear them, either, but I'm hard of hearing."

"You can say that again," Gorva said.

The high shaman's sagging jaw tightened. "Enough silly chatter. Kill the big ones. Leave the little one alive, and bring her to me. She'll talk as we feed her slowly to the Beast."

"If you lay a hand on her, we'll kill you all!" Razor warned.

"Our numbers are superior. You won't overcome us, thief!" Igmonbald replied. "Kill them!"

The hordes of lizard men rushed at them with blood in their eyes.

Rocks rained down from the sky, pelting the lizard men, stopping them in their tracks, and knocking them to the ground. They scrambled for cover near the bats.

"Those are some big hailstones," Razor said.

"That isn't hail." Zora pointed into the air. "It's the sky gnomes!"

Dozens of sky gnomes flew above, riding on the backs of their great vultures. They were led by Jumax on his griffon.

"Jumax!" Igmonbald roared. He shook his cudgel at the sky. "To the air! To the air!" He pointed at the lesser shaman who'd landed near him. "Lead the attack and kill the gnomes! I've got to release the Beast!"

The giant bats and their riders launched into the air and sped toward the sky gnomes. The bats and vultures collided in midair. Their talons ripped into flesh, and black feathers went flying.

Durmost soared right over Zora and said, "Watch this!" A moment later, he passed over a fleeing lizard man. The vulture's claws locked on the lizard man's shoulders and lifted him from the ground, then it carried the lizard man a hundred feet into the air and dropped him to his death on top of another lizard man. "Heee-heee! The Southern Storm has arrived!"

The gnomes attacked with small spears, and the lizard men used javelins made from solid wood. They jousted in the air like Monarch Knights. Bodies fell from the saddles. The nasty beasts of the air crashed from the heights.

Razor jumped away from a vulture that almost landed on top of him. He rolled from the ground to his feet. "Sweet Gapoli! It's raining chickens!"

Alarming cries and shrieking filled the air. A roar like a dragon's sounded.

Jumax's griffon locked its talons in the flesh of a giant bat and tore its wings off. The bat let out a pained shriek, and its wingless body torpedoed toward the ground.

Zora, Razor and Gorva became spectators of the gory battle above. The sky gnomes flung small weighted nets that tangled the bats' wings. The lizard men flung volley after volley of javelins, impaling vultures and gnomes. Wounded and bloody, both sides fought in a heated frenzy that rivaled any battle Zora had witnessed.

"They are berserk!" Zora stated. "I would never have imagined they'd fight like this."

"And it looks like those cuddly little gnomes are getting the better of the lizard skins." Razor scanned the area. "And I don't have anyone to fight. I'm missing my glory."

"Be happy you're still alive," Gorva said.

"Fighting is living for me," he replied. "Look!" He ducked.

The griffon glided over them and landed yards away. Jumax sat tall in the saddle. His dark skin gleamed in the sunlight, and his smile was wide. His beast walked toward them, stopped, and lay down. "Well done! You flushed out the enemy and silenced their shrieking plants, and now I can claim what is mine." His heavy stare scanned Zora from head to toe. "Where is the Ear of the Gods?"

"Oh," she said as she caught her breath. "It's hidden... er, in the gulch."

Jumax flung his hand up in a showy fashion and said, "Will you fetch it for me, little princess?"

Zora brushed her hair from her face and said, "Uh, certainly." She hurried to the gulch, grabbed the golden ear from its concealed spot, and ran back. She presented it to Jumax. "Here it is."

Jumax palmed the huge nugget and said, "Ah, it's as beautiful as I remember."

"What does it do?" Zora asked.

"It contains wondrous powers. Wondrous! But most of all..." He opened one of the griffon's saddlebags and dropped it inside. "It will look fantastic on my mantel."

Zora shared blank looks with Gorva and Razor. "Excuse me? We risked our lives so you could decorate your mantel?"

"That's one way of thinking about it." He winked at her and said, "But now your life debt has been repaid. You are free and have gained the faith and favor of Jumax and the Southern Storm. The Ear of the Gods will always serve as a reminder of your brazen heroics on the cactus field of battle." He lifted his muscular arms upward and spread out his hands. "Look! Be elated! Our enemy has been thwarted! All thanks to you!"

The lizard men fled on foot toward the Cliffs of the Beast. Their riders in the sky retreated as well.

"Their shrieking cacti are bred to detect us," Jumax continued. "Hence it was impossible to approach their den. Even when we're in the sky, they can sense us. Believe me... we have tried. But you... they were not ready for you." He grinned. "And you couldn't have come at a better time."

"Igmonbald mentioned the beast. He said that he would summon it," Zora warned.

Jumax raised an eyebrow. "Oh?"

Just then, the ground trembled. The top of the Cliffs of the Beast exploded, and a great monster crawled out and shrieked.

22

THE BEAST WAS every bit the size of a grand dragon, if not bigger, and it was a bat. It wasn't just any bat but one with bloodred skin and wings as black as coal. The top of its head was covered in coarse black hair that ran down and across its back. The tips of its wings ended in large hands with sharp claws that could snare a man whole. Its frightening shriek shook the dust up from the ground in waves of sound.

Jumax's mouth hung open. He closed it and said, "I've only heard the legends of the Beast, but none have ever seen it. The Beast is big. So big."

Before he could utter another word, the Beast leaped from the cliffs like it had been shot out of a ballista. It shredded the sky-gnome ranks and sent them tumbling in the air. Its clawed feet snatched a vulture and crushed its body until the bones popped. Then it turned and sped toward a sky gnome that was fleeing. Its jaws opened, and it swallowed the little man whole.

"Devastation!" Jumax shouted. "He gobbles up my people. Gorva, I need my spear." He climbed into the griffon's saddle and opened his hands. "Today I will become a legend, or I will find my rest in glory."

Spear in hand, Gorva climbed into the saddle behind him.

"What are you doing?" Jumax asked.

"Making sure you become a legend," she replied.

Jumax nodded and replied, "Today you will become a legend with me!" He gave a smoldering look and dug his heels into the griffon, and the beast launched itself into flight.

Razor moved beside Zora and said, "They're made for each other, aren't they?"

"I was thinking the same thing. Too bad Gorva won't realize it for another decade."

"Well, you know what they say. 'Those who fly together die together.'"

She eyed him. "I've never heard that before."

"No?" He watched the war in the winds. "Well, I'm sure it will come back to you."

Gorva's braids flapped in the wind, which was so loud that she had to shout above it. "Jumax, what is so special about this spear?"

"Haven't you noticed? That's why I gave it to you. The metal is blessed. It can pierce any flesh or metal," he hollered back.

They sped through the sky, chasing after the Beast that terrorized the sky gnomes.

"Why aren't we attacking?" she asked.

"We will, but I have to understand its patterns!" He leaned back into her. "It's been a long time since I've ridden with a woman. I missed the subtle pleasures of it."

"Focus on killing that monster before it eats all of your people."

"I can do both. After all, I'm a natural."

Gorva rolled her eyes but managed a smile. She wrapped her arms around Jumax's solid waist and held tight.

The griffon zigzagged through the sky, banking hard right and left, following on the tail of the twisting and turning bat.

"The Beast is clever! He chases one enemy only to veer away and surprise attack another! Ew!"

As predicted, the Beast broke its chase off of one sky gnome and banked hard into another, knocking the tiny man and great bird from the sky.

"I need to put an end to this!" Jumax reached back. "Give me the Spear of Jumax!"

She handed it to him and said, "You named it after yourself?"

"Of course. I own the Sword of Jumax and the other Sword of Jumax."

She patted his shoulder. "I understand."

He pulled back on the reins. The griffon rose high above the battle, wings pounding the air, and hovered.

Gorva clung to the saddle. "What are you doing?"

Jumax stared downward with an intense expression and said, "Grab the reins and come up here."

She climbed along his side, moving her back to his chest, and hung on.

"If I miss, don't mourn me." He gave her a passionate kiss, broke it off, and dove into the sky. "Glory! Glory!"

Gorva's heart skipped as she watched him descend to his death.

Zora let out a gasp.

"Holy horseshoes," Razor uttered. "He's bat-dung crazy."

Jumax had vaulted out of his saddle and descended spear-tip first toward the earth. He wasn't even lined up with the path of the Beast.

"He's going to miss by a league," Razor said. "I hope those wings aren't all show, because he's going to need them."

Zora sucked her teeth.

The Beast suddenly veered toward another sky gnome, on a path to where Jumax was descending.

Zora saw the whites of Jumax's eyes and his teeth gleaming in a grin. He speared the monster in the dead center of its back, and the point popped out of the other side.

The Beast shook. Its wings quaked, went limp, and flapped in the wind as its dead body plummeted to the earth. *Whomp!*

A huge cloud of dust rose from the spot where the Beast had planted.

"Jumax!" Zora started running toward the crash.

The griffon landed, and Gorva hopped off. She ran toward the cloud.

A wave of dust passed over them.

Zora covered her mouth with her scarf and said, "I can't see a thing."

Razor coughed. "Me either," he replied. "We need to wait for the dust to settle."

23

When the dust settled, Zora found Gorva sitting on the ground by the Beast cradling Jumax in her arms. His eyes were closed, and his face was smeared with blood. He didn't move as Gorva gently rocked him.

"Touching," Razor said quietly.

The sky gnomes chased the lizard men back to the cliffs. Igmonbald, the high shaman, was nowhere to be found.

Durmost, the sky gnome commander, joined Zora and Razor. His small face carried a worried expression, and his large, fuzzy ears wiggled. "Nooo. Nooo," he whined. He waddled over to Jumax, knelt, and placed his hands on the man's muscular thigh. "We won, but at what cost? Not our leader." He shook his fists in the air. "Not our magnificent leader!"

Word spread among the sky gnomes as they gathered closer and mourned. They screamed to the heavens and shed their woven suits of armor, crying out accolades in Jumax's name.

"A leader of leaders!"

"The most glorious of the glorious!"

"An all-father of the gnomes!"

"King of the friends!"

"The greatest warrior of all time!"

"The Beast Slayer!"

"The Beast Master!"

"A gallant knight who rules the sky with grace!"

"Thundermaster!"

"The Warrior of the Winds!"

"Wind Reaver!"

"The Scourge of Evil!"

Razor's head twisted from side to side as he surveyed the smaller people. "Sweet onions, they really worshipped this man. When I die, I want to be honored like that."

Gorva gave Razor a heavy look and asked, "Can you only think of yourself at a time such as this?"

"Since when did you become so smitten with him?" he replied with a shrug. "Sure, he's handsome, but you have to admit he was a bit lofty."

"The loftiest of the lofty!" Durmost blurted with tears streaming down his face.

Jumax's eyelids snapped open. His face was cradled in

Gorva's bosom, and in his strong voice, he said, "I like that one. And the view is even better."

Gorva's jaw dropped. She closed it with a snap and said, "You live!"

"Of course I live. I'm Jumax!"

Durmost let out a gleeful shout. "Jumax the Invincible!"

"What can I say? I'm an iron man," Jumax said with a shrug. Without any assistance, he stood and helped Gorva back to her feet. "All in a day's work."

"Jumax lives!" Word spread like wildfire among the sky gnomes, and they danced and shouted with jubilation.

"The Beast is dead, thanks to me." Jumax strolled over to the head of the Beast, which was taller than he was. His muscles rippled underneath his skin with every step. He placed his hand on the Beast's black snout. "This is one nasty creature. But I've defeated nastier." He climbed up the face of the Beast and found his spear then ripped it out of the Beast and held it above his head. "My people! My friends!"

The gnomes fell silent and looked up at him with bright eyes.

"The Southern Storm is victorious!"

The sky gnomes resumed their hooting and cheering. They danced arm in arm in circles. Even the ugly vultures began crowing.

Jumax jumped down to the ground and landed beside Gorva. "We will return to High Rock and celebrate our victory!" He wrapped one arm around Gorva's waist and pulled her in for a long kiss.

Razor and Zora shared surprised looks as they watched Gorva melt in Jumax's arms.

"And I will make you my bride!" Jumax announced when he broke the kiss off.

"What?" Gorva snapped out of her dreamlike state. "What did you say?"

"I said I will make you my bride. Imagine how glorious and beautiful our children will be!"

"You might be a great warrior and a great kisser but not good enough for me to bear your children." She ran her gaze from his head down to his toes and back up again. "Maybe in a few years, though."

"I'm disappointed," he said with a straight face. "You would be a welcome addition to my harem."

"*Harem?*" Gorva and Zora said in unison.

Jumax tossed his head back and roared with laughter. "I jest. I jest."

Zora caught him giving Razor a subtle wink.

"Who is your friend?" Jumax asked with a raised eyebrow as he looked behind Zora.

"What friend?" She glanced over her shoulder and nearly jumped out of her boots as she sprang backward into Jumax's chest. "Dalsay!"

Dalsay gave a polite nod and waved his hand in an arc. He wore the same dark-blue robes trimmed in arcane symbols that he always wore, but his body was in a see-through ethereal form. "It is good to see you," he said.

"You could have announced yourself," Zora said as she pulled free of Jumax's hand, which he'd fastened to her waist. "Where have you been?"

"At the Wizard Watch, communicating with Tatiana."

Zora approached him with wide eyes and asked, "How is she?"

"She is a survivor, but the underlings have not been making it easy. They are a vicious race." He tucked his hands into his robes and said, "I am looking for Grey Cloak. Where is he?"

"Not here, obviously," Razor said.

"Will you check for the Medallion of Location?" Dalsay asked. "I haven't been able to use my resources to find him."

"I've been looking, but I haven't had any luck." Zora opened Crane's satchel and removed the small jewel box. "Crane is dead. So are Jakoby and Leena."

Dalsay's form shimmered, and he said, "I am sorry to hear that. I know they were good friends."

"Don't you want to know what happened?" Razor asked.

"No," Dalsay replied. "That won't change anything."

Jumax brightened and said, "I want to know how they died. Was it a glorious battle or by a coward attack?"

"Glorious," Gorva muttered. "Their heroics saved us all."

Jumax gave a short pump of his fist. "We shall honor them."

Zora opened the jewel box while Dalsay peered over her shoulder. "See? Nothing. No, wait." A bright-green dot like a firefly's tail burned in the black bed of sand. "That's it."

"Well done. I know where that is."

Zora gave him a curious look and said, "How can you tell? It's only a bead in the sand that we follow."

"I'm a wizard. I know such things." He spread his hand over the jewel box. The sands turned into a map with very distinct markings of the world's terrain. "See? Lake Flugen and the trees of the Willowwacks. It appears they are in Oldham. Meet us there. I must go."

"But—"

Dalsay vanished into thin air.

"The dead wizard makes quite an entrance and exit. I like it," Jumax said with a broad smile. He took Gorva's hands in his and kissed her knuckles. "I take it our journey together ends here, eh, beautiful?"

"For now," she replied.

"Durmost! Take them where they need to go!" Jumax commanded.

24

OLDHAM

Grey Cloak, Dyphestive, and Anya landed in a stretch of forest southwest of Oldham. It was dusk, and the bright sun was setting behind the ridges, leaving them in the shade of the early evening. They climbed off of their dragons and stretched their legs.

Streak yawned, flexed his twin tails outward, and asked, "What are we landing for? Oldham is further north."

Twisting at the waist, Grey Cloak patted his dragon's snout and said, "You'll draw too much attention."

"I won't," Streak replied.

"No? You do realize that I flew on your back. It wasn't the other way around like it used to be."

Streak stretched out his wings and said, "Oh yeah, I'm not a runt anymore. Sometimes I forget I'm not a little guy. I miss it. Are you sure that I can't come?"

Grey Cloak shook his head.

Slicer, the dragon that Dyphestive had been riding, stood like a man and leaned against his father, Cinder. His slender talons were as sharp as knives and scraped together. "Let me come with you. I can be really subtle. And I'll watch your back."

Anya gave Cinder a doubtful look and asked, "Will you be able to control them while we're gone? It's their first time out in the wild, after all."

"No worries. I won't let them out of my sight," Cinder assured her. "You go and do what you must do, and we'll be awaiting your call if needed."

Anya cast a wary glance at the young dragons, who were milling about the bushes with their eyes wide. She donned a traveling cloak, patted Cinder on the nose, and said, "If you say so." She turned her attention to Grey Cloak. "Oldham might not look like much, but the last time we were here, the Black Guard was present, as well as a Risker."

Grey Cloak checked his weapons, adjusted the Cloak of Legends on his shoulders, and fastened the clasp under his chin. "Does the Risker ride a grand or a middling dragon?"

"Does it really matter?" Anya pulled her sky sword, weaved it through the air with flashing strikes, and snaked it back into her sheath. "Either way, I'll handle it."

Grey Cloak smirked. "Well, I guess we shall be underway." Scanning the grove, he asked, "Where's Dyphestive?"

"Over here," Dyphestive called. He appeared from the other side of Cinder with a quiver of thunder javelins over one shoulder and the iron sword in his free hand. "We're ready."

Feather walked behind him. She was loaded down with packs of weaponry, rations, and other gear. She even had a dragon helm wedged between her horns, sitting neatly on the top of her head.

Grey Cloak said, "Oh, I can see that. But we aren't laying siege to Oldham. This is a discrete mission."

Dyphestive's broad shoulders sagged.

Feather's head dipped, and her pink eyes looked sad.

"Can I take my sword?" Dyphestive asked.

"That claymore? I don't think that's such a good idea. Of course, you are more than welcome to stay here and keep the dragons company," Grey Cloak suggested, even though he didn't wish to be alone with Anya.

Dyphestive stuck his sword into the ground and loaded the quiver of thunder javelins on Feather. "Sorry. Maybe next time, sister."

"Grab a cloak," Anya said.

"More like a curtain," Grey Cloak commented. He turned to Anya. "Lead the way."

Anya nodded and began the march to Oldham with her wavy locks bouncing behind her shoulders.

"So, tell us more about your friend the wizard... or Oldham, for that matter," Grey Cloak said.

"I told you... Atticus is unique. And Oldham is ancient. That is all you need to know," Anya said. She broke free of the forest line, and nothing but open grasslands and rolling hills were ahead. "Try to keep pace. I won't be slowing."

"Of course not. After all, you seem very eager to see Atticus." He caught Dyphestive giving him a look of warning and shrugged it off. "Does Atticus live in the city? Does he have a tower?"

"I told you. He'll find us. We need to be patient. You are the one that wishes to exercise discretion. Why would Atticus be any different? As I told you, he is unique. If anyone knows a way into the Wizard Watch, it will be him."

"If you say so." Grey Cloak slowed his pace and drifted back to his brother. "Don't you find it odd that she trusts a wizard?"

"Of course, but what choice to we have?" Dyphestive replied.

"Remember what Rhonna used to say? There's more than one way to skin a giant."

Dyphestive nodded. "I always liked that saying."

"Well, stay alert until we can get a good feel about Atticus. It all seems very suspicious to me."

"But you know we can trust Anya, right?"

"Yes, but do you remember how Tatiana was fooled by the Wizard Watch and what that led to?"

"I do."

"Besides, there is something else I've been contemplating the last several days. But keep it to yourself."

"Really? What?" Dyphestive asked.

"The whereabouts of the Helm of the Dragons."

25

THE WELL-TRAVELED cobblestone streets of Oldham were riddled with deep potholes that tripped two drunken laborers, who fell to the ground. One hauled the other one up, only to back into another pothole and tumble. His jug of wine burst, and he let out an angry shout.

Grey Cloak giggled. "I can see why you like this place, Anya. It's a good fit for your temperament."

Dyphestive scanned the building tops. The old structures had wooden shingles on their tall towers and steep roofs. Bats darted across the street, devouring fireflies with bright-orange tails. The evening breeze carried a rotten smell across the roads, and every building creaked and groaned.

Grey Cloak tapped his brother on the shoulder and said, "Try not to look like a stranger."

"How old is this place?" Dyphestive asked with avid fascination.

"They say that Oldham was the original capitol of Gapoli, long before the first stone was ever laid in Monarch City," Anya replied.

"I've never heard that," Dyphestive replied.

"Again, *they*, as in the citizens of Oldham say that. Their truth is what they say it is."

"Humph," Dyphestive uttered.

They moved down the right side of the road, staying in the shadows of the porch fronts and buildings. Many people were about, men and orcs mostly, but a few halflings and dwarves could be seen inside the tavern windows and wandering from one side of the street to the other. Their loose-fitting dress was in poor condition, and most of them walked on bare feet or sandals.

Several men and women leaned against the porch posts, smoking pipes and cigars and talking quietly. None of them said a word when Grey Cloak, Anya, and Dyphestive passed by.

Black Guard patrolled the streets. They walked on foot with their steel helmets catching the torch- and moonlight. Their red tunics over chain-mail dress could be clearly seen. They paid no attention to Grey Cloak, Anya, and Dyphestive as they casually made their way deeper into the bowels of the old city.

Shriek!

The spine-chilling dragon call was sudden and loud. A great dragon soared across the sky and passed under the bright white moon.

"That's a grand," Grey Cloak said to Anya. "I thought you said it was a middling."

"It *was* a middling. Who is to say that they can't change their guard?"

"That was a big grand. Did you see his belly?" Dyphestive added. "He looked bigger than Cinder."

Two more dragons darted after the huge one.

"Middlings!" Grey Cloak exclaimed quietly. "A pair, at that. I'm not certain meeting your friend Atticus is a wise course of action. If they see—"

"They won't see our dragons. No doubt Cinder has heard that flying watermelon by now. He knows how to hide. After all, it's not the first time we've evaded enemy dragons."

"Yes, when it was the two of you. Now we are seven."

"Don't panic and come along." She cut into a narrow alley and spooked a pair of green-eyed cats. At the end of the alley was a doorway with an old orc sitting on a barrel outside of it.

The orc had a hump on his back, and his eyes were droopy. He scanned their faces and hammered the wooden door with his ham-sized fist. He opened his fist. "Three chips."

Anya looked at Grey Cloak.

He fished three silver chips out of his purse and dropped them into the orc's greasy palm.

The orc wiped his running nose and said, "Three chips apiece!"

"*Apiece?*"

"Pay him," Anya said.

With a sigh, Grey Cloak obliged.

The door opened, and they were nearly knocked over by the smell of sweat.

Grey Cloak covered his nose and moved aside. "Ladies first."

Anya entered the dimly lit establishment and nearly vanished in the darkness. Dyphestive followed her, and Grey Cloak took one last look down the alley before he entered. He found Anya and Dyphestive sitting on barstools, ordering drinks at the bar. They were being served by a young woman with straight jet-black hair cut at the shoulders. The barmaid's bangs almost hid her eyes completely. She smiled and set three pints before them then departed into the kitchen.

Aside from the three of them, no one else was inside the quaint tavern, which smelled like moldy wood.

Grey Cloak suddenly realized that no one had opened the door from the inside. The hair on his neck rose as he sat down beside Anya and asked, "Who let us in?"

She shrugged and started drinking her ale. "Don't worry about it."

A fire burned in a small fireplace in the corner of the room. The dry wood cracked and popped.

Dyphestive's stool groaned every time he moved. He put his lips to the rim of his glass and sipped. "This is good," he commented.

"Have some," Anya said to Grey Cloak. "We might be here a while."

Grey Cloak scanned the room. Cobwebs hung in the lofty corners, and spiders of all sorts scurried over the rafters. All of the tables were round, and a red candle in a brass candleholder was lit on top of each of them. "Not the sort of place I'd expect to meet a wizard. Why here?"

"He told me if I need him, this would be the place to come." She finished her ale and pushed it forward. "And this is where we should wait."

The barmaid appeared from behind the swinging doors that led to the kitchen. She wiped her hands on a rag and asked them, "Would you like another?"

"Please," Anya said.

Dyphestive let out a long belch and said, "Definitely."

The barmaid smiled and asked Grey Cloak, "You aren't drinking?"

"Not as fast as them, apparently." He lifted his pint and said, "I'm still working on it."

"Drink all that you want," someone with a clear, strong voice said. "I'm paying for it."

All three of them turned and faced a man who had appeared out of thin air.

Anya hopped off of her stool and threw her arms around him. "Atticus!"

26

ATTICUS DIDN'T MEET the unique description that Anya had given them. He was a striking human, older than they were by a few years, tall, lean, and well built, with neatly cut short hair turning gray above the ears. He offered a charming smile. His chin was strong and his mannerisms polished, and he caressed Anya's back in a manner that she didn't appear to mind.

He wore a set of brick-red wizard robes that had a high collar and were sleeveless, showing his sinewy arms. An ornate pair of bronze bracers that were encrusted with rubies that twinkled with living fire adorned his arms above the wrists.

When Grey Cloak's eyes traveled down Atticus's body, he didn't see the man's feet.

Odd. I didn't even hear him come in. What is so unique about him? Sure, he's good-looking, but he's not elf good-looking.

Atticus broke off his embrace with Anya, offered his hand to Grey Cloak, and said, "I'm Atticus. Welcome."

Grey Cloak shook the man's hand, surprised by his iron grip, and said, "Thank you. I didn't hear you come in. How'd you—"

"Whoa, look at this big fella," Atticus said as he moved on to Dyphestive. He felt Dyphestive's massive arms. "Lords of Iron, what do you eat?"

Dyphestive shook his hand and said, "Everything."

Atticus bit down on his lip as he shook Dyphestive's hand. "Your grip is incredible. Like an ogre's." He pulled his hand away and shook it. "I think he broke my hand. Only jesting. Come, everyone, grab your pints and sit down by the fire." He moved to a table near the fireplace.

"Unique, huh?" Grey Cloak whispered to Anya.

"Yes, in his own sort of way."

"If I didn't know any better, I'd say you're smitten."

She twirled a strand of her hair around her finger. "Oh, don't be silly." She took her seat beside Atticus at a table for four.

Grey Cloak sat across from him. Dyphestive's chair creaked the moment he sat down.

"Poor chair," Atticus commented. "It wasn't created for a man of your girth. Here, let me strengthen it before it collapses." He leaned over and grabbed the chair leg, and the bracers on his arms glowed like burning embers. "There, that ought to do it. Wiggle around."

Dyphestive rocked his hips and smiled. "Not a creak or a groan. How'd you do that?"

Atticus held his hands up. "It's my gift... well, one of many." He grabbed Anya's hand. "I am so pleased to see you again. You are as gorgeous as ever."

"I'm sure the years haven't been as kind as you say. Life on the run has been difficult, to say the least," she said as her cheeks turned rosy. "You are looking as well as ever. Very well."

"Ah, you flatter me. Look at my locks." He ran his fingers through his hair. "I'm almost gray. I'm too young to be gray like an old man."

"It's a shame," Grey Cloak commented. "But you know what they say. Time ages everyone, especially the old."

"Indeed." Atticus didn't take his eyes off of Anya as he said, "Well, tell me, why are you here? I can only imagine that it is an urgent matter, or you wouldn't have risked coming to see me."

"We need to find a way into the Wizard Watch tower in Arrowwood," she said.

"Oh." Atticus leaned back in his chair, and his friendly face became a mask of concentration. "You know I'm not in league with those devils and their ivory towers."

Anya gave Grey Cloak an "I told you so" look.

Atticus tapped his fingertips together and said, "As I understand it, the Wizard Watch is being controlled by otherworldly powers." He sneered. "They had it coming, if you ask me. It's the price you pay for neutrality. They always sided with where the wind blew strongest. Pathetic." He regained his smile. "Apologies. But we have a history that goes back... well, a very long time."

"I can imagine, at your age," Grey Cloak replied.

"Oh, no, you can't," Atticus stated. "No, you can't."

Anya kicked Grey Cloak in the ankle.

"Can you get us inside or not?" Grey Cloak asked.

"That is a very dangerous request. Why do you want inside the Wizard Watch?" Atticus asked.

Grey Cloak leaned forward and said, "That's our business."

Anya glared at Grey Cloak and said, "Don't be rude. He's on our side. And we are his guests. Tell him why."

"Pardon?"

"You should do as you're ordered. It's for the best," Atticus suggested.

Grey Cloak tapped his chest and said, "You have it all wrong. I give the orders."

"Is that so?" Atticus asked Anya.

"Yes," she said through clenched teeth.

"Interesting." Atticus rubbed his hands together. "You

are very young. All of you are. But I am sorry to say, in this matter, I cannot help you."

"Why not?" Grey Cloak demanded.

"The answer is simple." He eyed Grey Cloak. "I don't like you."

27

"WELL DONE, Grey Cloak. Well done indeed," Anya stated. "How are we supposed to find a way into the Wizard Tower now?"

They were standing outside of Atticus's tavern, and the door was closed.

"I'll think of—"

"Something!" Anya punched the door. "I'm tired of hearing that. Atticus is a friend, and you insulted him."

"I didn't insult him. A man of his maturity shouldn't be that thin-skinned."

"Do you mind?" the orc sitting by the door asked. He waved them away. "You're blocking the entrance."

They all peered down the empty alley and slowly moved away from the door.

"I can't believe you." Anya shook her head. "You were

rude to him. And we're short of help. You know that, don't you? We need allies."

He looked at his brother. "Dyphestive, was I rude?"

"Yes. Jealous, if you ask me," Dyphestive replied.

"I didn't ask you that, did I?" Grey Cloak sighed. He didn't know what had gotten into him, but watching Atticus fawn over Anya had struck a chord that he didn't want to admit. "If it makes you feel better, I'll apologize to the old man."

"Old man? See? There you go again with the insults." Anya threw her hands up. "This is why I should be leading. Not you."

"Why not me?"

She poked him in the chest. "Because you are immature. That's why!"

He got nose to nose with her. "And you're a hothead!"

"Can we not do this now? We have more important matters to focus on besides your blossoming affection for one another," Dyphestive said.

The orc chuckled.

Grey Cloak and Anya quickly separated.

"Listen, let me try to talk with Atticus alone," she said in a lowered voice. "I think it's better that way. Give me an hour."

"Works for me," Grey Cloak said.

The orc banged on the door. It swung silently inward.

Anya disappeared back inside, and the door shut behind her.

"Well, that's that." Grey Cloak started down the alley. "Let's take a walk."

Dyphestive caught up to him and said, "You know, I liked Atticus. I'm not sure why you didn't."

"I was only vetting him. And we can't be too careful these days. And I don't think Anya is any better a judge of people than we are. Do you?"

Dyphestive shrugged. "I suppose not." He looked behind him. "Do you think it's safe, leaving her with him?"

"We'll know soon enough. Let's find something to eat." He patted his belly. "We haven't had a good meal in quite some time."

"I like the sound of that and the smell of greasy food. Mmm... I can taste it already."

They took a right after they exited the alley and moved quickly down the street. There were several taverns to choose from in the old and large city, which rivaled Raven Cliff in size, if not even greater.

Dyphestive laid his hand on Grey Cloak's shoulder and pointed at a hanging wooden sign that read: The Potbellied Orc Inn. "That looks like my kind of place." He drew a deep breath through his nose. "Mmm, bacon."

"No need to start drooling all over yourself. At least wait until you get a bib."

They were about to walk up the stairs to the entrance to

the inn when an icy breeze came down the street. The hairs on Grey Cloak's nape stood on end. He turned and saw a bright-red door across the street that slowly began to open. He hooked Dyphestive by the arm and said, "I have a bad feeling about this."

Dyphestive's eyes were fixed on the inn, and he said, "What? It smells wonderful."

Giant-sized purple tentacles burst out of the front door of Batram's Bartery and Arcania and wrapped around Grey Cloak's and Dyphestive's waists. The tentacles effortlessly jerked them into the store, and the door slammed shut behind them.

"Welcome!" the gruff-voiced boar's-head rug stated loudly. "Be sure to wipe your feet!"

The tentacles were nowhere to be seen as they stared down at the boar's-head rug.

Dyphestive absentmindedly started wiping his boots on the rug.

"Ooh!" the boar's head said. "That feels good!"

Batram's Bartery and Arcania had not changed in the slightest. A grand display case with glass windows and blackwood trim stood in the front of the store, with beautiful baubles and artifacts within. Behind the counter were drawers and shelving that ran to the heights of the tall ceiling. Spiderwebs covered the nooks and crannies, and the tiny spiders could be seen crawling or nesting everywhere. Batram sat on the top of the display case in halfling form with his legs hanging over the side. His hair and sideburns were like cotton, and he wore a striped white-and-black jacket with a red flower in the front pocket. The shrewd negotiator revealed a smile of razor-sharp teeth and said, "I've been looking for you."

"Thank you for seeing me again," Anya said to Atticus. She joined him in the same spot in the tavern where they'd sat before. "Grey Cloak is difficult."

"No need to apologize." Atticus patted her hand. "I expect a certain degree of arrogance from a natural. After all, it takes one to know one, right?"

"I don't think he realized you were one."

Atticus leaned back in his chair and shrugged. "He's young, and clearly he cares for you very much, or he wouldn't have acted out that way. I can't say I blame him."

"If you are suggesting that he is fond of me, you are sadly mistaken. You should have been there when he tried to kick my skull in."

He chuckled. "He's clever. Like his mother."

"You knew Zanna Paydark?"

"Quite well. Even though she led the life of a Sky Rider, she kept up relationships with outcasts like me. She was wise. I see a lot of her in her son." He drummed on the table and said, "So, you would like to enter the Wizard Watch, and you require my assistance, eh?"

She nodded. "Correct."

"If that is the case, I'm going to need you to fill me in on a few more details." With his elbows on the table, he leaned forward, offered a devilish smile, and added, "And by a few details, I mean everything you know."

28

GREY CLOAK LOOKED at the halfling sitting on the display counter and said, "It's good to see you, too, Batram. Are those new boots? Very eye-catching."

"Hello, Batram." Dyphestive wiggled his fingers in the air. "It's been a long time."

Batram crinkled his button nose and replied, "Oh, don't worry. You'll be seeing plenty of me if you don't have what I'm looking for." He narrowed his dark eyes and scanned Dyphestive and Grey Cloak. "Where is it?"

Grey Cloak leaned his shoulder against the tall display case and asked, "Where is what?"

"The Sword of Chaos." Batram hopped on top of the display case and paced from one end to the other. "I don't see the sword. Where is the sword?" he demanded.

Dyphestive tilted his head over his shoulder and asked, "What sword?"

"Pfft! Don't pretend you don't know. I made a deal with your brother. I gave him the location of the Figurine of Heroes, and in exchange, he was going to retrieve for me the Sword of Chaos."

"The iron sword?" Dyphestive asked Grey Cloak.

"There were many swords in the treasure vault of Thannis, Batram, and we barely made it out alive," Grey Cloak said. He eyed the treasures inside the glass display case—ornate sets of daggers, jewel-encrusted rings, necklaces made from precious jewels of all sorts, tiaras with sparkling emeralds, a full metal helmet with a drop-down vizor, and a crown with six horns, each with a different gem on the tip. "And it appears that you are doing well."

"Don't play games with me, Grey Cloak. I tire of your chitter-chatter. I'm not a common street merchant that you can hustle." Batram dropped behind the counter and rose on the other side in the form of a ten-foot-tall monster with a spider's head, large pitch-black eyes, eight spidery arms, and the same striped coat. "You are in my abode now, and only I can allow you to leave. I can trap you here for decades. For centuries." He leaned over the counter and glowered at Grey Cloak. "You wouldn't want that. Would you?"

"It depends. Will you be feeding us?"

"And if so, what will you be serving?" Dyphestive asked. "Not that I'm particular, but I do enjoy trying the garden variety of meat."

Batram drummed his twenty spidery fingers on the counter and said through his sharp clenched teeth, "My patience thins."

"What is so important about the Sword of Chaos?" Grey Cloak asked.

"That's my business." Batram waved his right set of arms across the display case. An image of the Sword of Chaos appeared and hovered above the glass. It was an exact replica of the iron sword, with a square-cut ruby nesting in the pommel. He studied Dyphestive's face and asked, "Is this the sword you carry?"

Dyphestive's mouth hung open, and he nodded.

"*Where is it?*" Batram demanded. The image of the sword faded. "I need it!"

"What do you want for it?" Dyphestive asked. "I want to keep it."

"The price is too high for you to pay, boy."

"No price is too high," Grey Cloak said with a smile. "Come on, Batram. This is what we do. We barter. We exchange. Certainly, there is something else of value that we can fetch for you."

Batram folded the lower half of his arms across his chest and cupped his big chin underneath two of his hands. "So, you want another mission, even though you have yet to fulfill this one. Ha!" He scratched his cheek. "But I have an idea. Hand over the Figurine of Heroes, and we'll consider our matters settled."

Grey Cloak casually wrapped himself in his cloak and said, "You know I can't do that. We need the figurine to banish the underlings."

"That is not a matter of concern in my line of work. People come to me to find an edge over the other. Many times they are desperate. Often, they don't make it back to reclaim what they left." Batram ran some of his strange hands across the top of the glass. "Then the treasure is mine to do what I please with. I can trade it, sell it, or use it for collateral."

"I understand how it works." Grey Cloak snared several objects they'd gotten from the vault inside the Ruins of Thannis. He rummaged through his pockets and produced a stubby golden idol with large teeth. "How about this?"

"I like the way it shines, but it is not something that I desire. Perhaps you need to rethink your strategy when it comes to dealing with the underlings. Why don't you give the Figurine of Heroes to me and use the Sword of Chaos to destroy them?"

"I like the sound of that," Dyphestive said. "But if I can get ahold of them, I can kill them with my bare hands. Keep the figurine, brother. I'll fetch the sword and give it to him."

Grey Cloak shook his head. "No, brother, you love that

sword. I don't think you should have to part with it." He fished a blue sapphire from his pocket and held it up.

Batram's big eyes reflected the bright charm. He wrung his hands and leaned closer. His voice took on a hungry tone. "The Eye of Enthrallment. I sold that to Drysis the Dreadful. How did you come to possess it?"

"We killed her and took it," Grey Cloak said.

"I didn't know you had that," Dyphestive commented.

Grey Cloak focused his attention on Batram. "This is a very strong artifact. It can reveal the truth from a lie. Any man or any woman would die to have such power."

"So long as they'll sacrifice their eye for it." Batram clacked his teeth. "And pay a large fortune." He licked his teeth with his slimy black tongue. "I'll strike a deal with you. Give me the Eye, and I will let you keep the sword."

"This is a sudden turn, even for you, Batram." Grey Cloak tossed the gemstone up and caught it. "Clearly the eye is of greater value than the sword."

Batram's face contorted with rage. "It is not!" He took a swipe at the gem.

Grey Cloak hopped backward out of reach and made the gem vanish with a sleight of hand. "That wasn't very nice, Batram."

"Whatever gave you the idea that I'm nice? Hmm? I don't trade to come out behind, but ahead, you fools. Look at me. Look at my treasure." He spread all eight of his arms out wide. "I am the god of my world, and you are my guest! What will it be, Grey Cloak? Will you trade with me, or will you never leave?"

29

ATTICUS LEANED back in his chair, sawing his index figure underneath his lip. He had a small smile on his face and hadn't said a word in minutes. His clear eyes picked up Anya's reflection.

Anya rubbed her clammy palms on her thighs. She'd never been nervous around anyone, but for some reason, Atticus gave her butterflies. He had more to him than good looks and a casual charm, but she couldn't put her finger on it. For some reason, she felt comfortable telling him everything—perhaps too comfortable, and she felt guilty.

"Ahem," she said. "Do you mind telling me what you're thinking?"

Atticus took a sudden breath through his nose and blinked. He managed a charming laugh and said, "Apologies. I departed briefly. It was rude of me."

She gave him a curious look. "Departed?"

"It's part of my craft called wizard's intuition. I have an extraordinary sense of my surroundings. A very strong being entered Oldham." His voice darkened. "There is danger here. You should go."

"Wait. What about the Wizard Watch? Can you tell us a way to get in?"

He shook his head. "I fear that I cannot, Anya."

"What? But I told you everything."

"I know." He kissed her hand. "You have trusted me, and I am honored. That is why I am telling you that you must go now. There is danger. Get as far away from Oldham as you can before it's too late."

Anya knocked her chair over when she jumped to her feet. "You snake! I give you my trust, and in return, you give me less than I had when I came."

"I wouldn't expect you to understand. But you must find your friends and leave now."

A breeze whooshed through the dingy room, and the tavern door opened wide. An unseen force pulled Anya toward the door. She turned her gaze back to Atticus. The wizard was gone.

"Cretin!"

She was whisked off of her feet and landed outside on her backside. The alley was empty. The orc doorkeeper was gone, and the old door had been replaced by a wall. Feeling like a fool, she stood and cursed. "I hate wizards."

A dark shadow passed over the alley. *Skreee!*

She jogged to the end of the alley and nearly ran into Grey Cloak and Dyphestive. The three of them came to an abrupt halt.

She marched right by them and said, "We need to go."

"Whoa, what's the hurry?" Grey Cloak caught up with her. "And where is your dear friend Atticus?"

"He's gone. But not without a warning. He said we need to leave."

"But he told you a way to get into the Wizard Watch, right?" Grey Cloak asked.

She shook her head.

Grey Cloak grabbed her by the elbow and stopped her. "He didn't tell you anything? Nothing at all?"

She jerked her arm away. "What difference does it make? We took a chance. It didn't pay. I guess you'll have to *think of something.*"

Grey Cloak shared concerned looks with Dyphestive and asked her, "What does he know?"

"What do you mean?"

"I mean what did you tell him about us? Our mission? The figurine?"

Anya's cheeks were burning when she said, "Everything."

"Oh, well, if that's all. No worries. I mean, everything isn't that much, it's only... *everything!*"

"Lower your voice, you fool!" she said as she looked

down the street, where some figures lingering in the shadows of the porches began to gather. "Trust me. We need to go." She pushed past him.

Grey Cloak joined his brother, followed her, and said, "Be ready for anything."

"I am," Dyphestive said. "I am."

Anya had never felt like such an idiot in all of her life. Grey Cloak was right. She'd been smitten and smitten by a wizard, of all things. She'd given Atticus their plans to invade the Wizard Watch disguised as Doom Riders. Not only that, but she'd also revealed that they were in possession of the Figurine of Heroes. Her stupidity sent fiery chills straight through her. And worst of all, none of it would have happened if she'd only been willing to follow Grey Cloak's lead.

Grey Cloak caught up with her and said, "Anya, do you think it's possible that Atticus might be in league with the other side?"

"Of course not. Just because he doesn't know a way into the Wizard Watch doesn't mean that he serves the enemy," she said adamantly.

He replied, "It doesn't mean he doesn't either. Be honest. Do you think he might be a traitor to our cause?"

She stopped and said, "I'm not such a fool that I cannot rule it out. Does that help? What do you want me to admit? That I erred?"

Grey Cloak raised his palms. "Even if you did, and you

probably did, we are in this together." He set his eyes on the road ahead, which led south out of the city. "But now it's time to cut our losses and go."

His calming words took some of the fire out of Anya. She nodded and said, "After you."

They hurried out of the city without encountering a single soldier from the Black Watch. Even the dragon calls in the heavens were silent as they followed the road toward the black hills where they'd left their friends.

Grey Cloak slowed to a stop and took a knee. Without pointing, he asked quietly, "Do you see that?"

A large black hump blocked the road.

Anya replied, "I see it."

Dyphestive stuck his head between theirs and added, "So do I."

The dark bulk came to life and huffed out a plume of fire, revealing a grand dragon. It set the ground aflame, turning the dark into day. As the flames rose higher, two more middling dragons appeared on each side of the great beast. One man came forward, a heavyset Risker with a scalp that was as bald as an egg. He opened his arms wide and said with rugged glee, "I'll be. It's my old friends Dindae and Festive."

30

GREY CLOAK FELT Dyphestive bristle beside him as an old acquaintance, the broadly built Commander Slaught, approached. The hairs on his arms rose when he looked the Risker in the face. Commander Slaught's flat nose looked like it had been smashed in with a hammer. He wore a full suit of plate-mail armor—bulging in the belly— that made him appear huge and even more imposing.

"What's the matter, Dindae? Festive?" Commander Slaught asked in his gruff voice. "Don't you have any kind words to share with your former trainer?"

"Who is he talking about?" Anya asked as she drew her sword. "Who are Dindae and Festive?"

"That's us. Our real names," Grey Cloak admitted. "From a long time ago."

"Oh, it hasn't been that long. Maybe fifteen years or so."

Commander Slaught spat tobacco juice on the ground. "Time goes by fast." His metal fingers danced on the pommel of a long sword strapped to his hip. He eyed Anya. "So, you must be the last Sky Rider. Anya, isn't it?"

"You figured that out all by yourself. Bravo," she said.

Commander Slaught stuck his big chin out and chuckled. "She has an attitude. I like it. A shame I didn't have a chance to train her instead of the pair of you. You know..." He spat again. "I took a lot of heat when you escaped. A lot. But now it looks like I'll get a chance to redeem myself."

"Come now, Commander, you don't want the sort of trouble that we bring," Grey Cloak said. "Why don't you pretend that you never saw us? Let us go about our business. We won't say a word, and no one, especially you, will have to die today."

"Listen to you! You speak like a man with steel in his spine. I'm proud of you. That's how I train my Riskers to be." Commander Slaught rubbed his chin and eyed Dyphestive. "And look at Festive. Full grown and mighty. Are you still as dull as a river stone?"

"No, I'm duller," Dyphestive said.

Commander Slaught laughed. "How about that? He found a scrap of personality. Listen, we can do this the easy way or the hard way. You can surrender and come quietly, or we'll kill the lot of you."

"Is there a third option?" Grey Cloak asked.

"I think he left out the option that we kill him," Dyphestive stated.

"Agreed," Anya said.

Commander Slaught stood equidistant from them, his dragon, and the other two Riskers, who were still mounted on their middling dragons. "Do you hear that, Fredrake? These adepts think they can defeat us. Us! Huh-huh-huh." The sweat on his bald head glistened in the moonlight, and he added, "Fredrake, come closer and say hello to our old friends."

The dragon behind Commander Slaught rose. Fredrake had two short horns pointing outward like a bull's. His long, thick neck was layered with heavy scales. His eyes burned with green from within, and more green scales made tortoiseshell patterns over the rest of his dark-scaled body. He lowered his massive head over Commander Slaught, and a long black tongue flicked out of his mouth like a lash. "Yes, I remember them," he said in a raspy voice. "The striplings have grown. How delicious they will be with the extra meat on their bones."

"Hello, Fredrake. Judging by the extra bulk you're carrying, I think you've been eating as well as Commander Slaught," Grey Cloak quipped.

The full-blooded grand dragon demanded and received respect in the dragon kennels of Dark Mountain. Grey Cloak wondered why they'd been posted at a city as dead as Oldham. "How many cattle a day are you gobbling up? Ten? Twenty?"

"I'm going to eat you piece by piece," the massive dragon hissed.

Grey Cloak smirked. "Are we still negotiating? Or is this a reunion? I can't help but wonder, why are you here? Did Dirklen and Magnolia have something to do with this? Was this your punishment for losing us? Is this how Black Frost put both of you fat lumps of troll dung out to pasture? Was it this or death?"

Commander Slaught hollered, "Silence! Never mention those fair-haired fools to me again."

"Sounds like you hit a sore spot," Dyphestive said.

"Who? Me?" Grey Cloak replied.

Commander Slaught's hard stare bore into Grey Cloak. "You never could bridle that sharp tongue of yours, could you, elf? Today, I will cut it out!" He pulled his long sword, a well-crafted blade that shone like molten silver. "Kill them! Kill them all!"

31

"SPLIT UP, EVERYONE!" Grey Cloak jumped backward, avoiding Commander Slaught's sword tip.

Dyphestive dashed to the left, and Anya went right. They attacked the Riskers mounted on the middlings.

Grey Cloak summoned the wizard fire, and the Rod of Weapons bloomed with a spear tip of blue fire.

"That's pretty. What do you plan to do? Poke me in the eye with it?" Commander Slaught asked. He charged at full speed and crashed his sword into the Rod of Weapons. Magic sizzled on impact. He thrust, cut, and stabbed again.

Grey Cloak parried every jarring strike and took a couple of quick pokes at Slaught's eyes.

Commander Slaught battered the rod away with a strong backswing and laughed. "You're fast. I'll give you that. But you aren't a seasoned veteran like me."

Commander Slaught reached over his shoulder and grabbed a small round buckler that was attached to his back. He summoned his own wizard fire into it. It bloomed with quavering green light, and he marched forward like an ox and said, "I'm going to cut you to ribbons!"

Without thinking, Dyphestive set his eyes on the Risker to his right and charged the man and his dragon like a bull. He leaped over Fredrake's sweeping tail and collided into the middling dragon's chest.

The beast spat up a plume of fire. The Risker in the saddle pulled on the reins and hollered, "Settle down! Settle down!" He grabbed a javelin and stuck it in the meat of Dyphestive's shoulder. "Death to you, vermin!"

Dyphestive grabbed the man by the wrist with one hand and punched him in the side of his metal helmet with the other. The man's teeth clacked.

The Risker wobbled in the saddle. His body sagged, and he tumbled out of the saddle and fell hard onto the ground.

Dyphestive pulled the javelin out of his shoulder and slung it to the dirt, just missing the Risker. He pumped his fist in the air and grabbed the dragon's reins.

The middling dragon coiled its tail around Dyphestive's

neck and yanked him hard out of the saddle then slammed him into the ground.

Dyphestive wrestled for his life, grabbing the tail and trying to peel it free.

The dragon's tail constricted like a python, cutting off his breath. The beast pulled Dyphestive under it and pinned him down with its talons. Its face came nose to nose with Dyphestive's. Its hot breath burned his cheeks, and burning saliva dripped onto his face.

On shaky arms, the Risker crawled over to Dyphestive. The man had a hard look about him and evil in his eyes. He said, "At least you got one good shot in before you die." He patted his dragon's snout and stood on trembling legs. He stroked the dragon charm, which burned like a flame inside the chest plates of his armor. "But now I am going to watch you burn alive. Torch him!"

"So, you are the last of the Sky Riders?" an orcen Risker asked Anya. He sat tall in his saddle, showing off his slender build and long arms. He carried a long spear with a fiery tip. His middling dragon's head moved in whatever direction Anya went. "I am Roffik. You should know the name of the man who is about to slay you."

"That's easier said than done," she replied. "You should ask the other men what happened when they tried to slay me. Oh, but you can't. They're dead!" She took a running leap, sailed high over the dragon's snapping jaws, and took a midair swing at Roffik's spear. The weapons clashed hard, and she landed behind the dragon.

The dragon flicked its tail at her. She ducked and chopped off the end with her blazing-hot steel. The dragon shuffled around and shot at her with a blast of fire.

Anya jumped out of the path of the flames, did a somersault, and popped back up to her feet. She found herself flanked by the enemy. Roffik faced her on one side, and the dragon hemmed her in on the other.

"You picked a beautiful night to die, Anya," Roffik said with a cocky grin. He rolled the tip of his spear in a circle and built up speed. "Though you can always surrender, and I'll make your life easy."

"I would never have made it this far if I surrendered every time I fought," she said.

"Well, this will be your last stop." Roffik's spear let out a high-pitched whine, and a bolt of energy shot out of the tip.

Anya brought up her sword to block, but she was a wink too late. The missile of energy hit her full in the chest and knocked her to the ground.

The middling dragon scurried toward her with its head low, jaws half open, and pounced. It landed on top of Anya and started tearing away at her with its claws.

She fought it off with her fists and blocked it with her dragon armor. She snaked out a dagger and punched a hole in its gut. It pressed its full weight on her, crushing her underneath its scaly, horse-sized body, and started to crush her.

Roffik took a knee, stared at her pinned body, and said, "It's going to be a shame to watch you die, Anya. A real pity. I've never slain a woman like you before."

32

ZOOKS, he's good!

Using the Rod of Weapons like a spear, Grey Cloak was walked backward by the force of Commander Slaught's sheer power. He quickly learned that the commander wasn't an ordinary man but a full-blooded natural born with superhuman strength. He parried his sword strikes, and his quick jabs were blocked by Slaught's shield.

"You should never have smarted off to me. I could have made your life easy!" Commander Slaught said as he whipped his sword downward in a skull-splitting strike.

Grey Cloak skipped left and stabbed at Slaught's feet.

The commander sprang away with the agility of a large cat. He turned on Grey Cloak and came at him full force with a series of lightning-quick blows.

Grey Cloak blocked, dodged, ducked, and leaped out of the man's dangerous path, backpedaling.

He's as strong as a bull! As fast as a snake. Think, Grey Cloak. Think!

Commander Slaught backed off, stood in the tall grass, spat out a mouthful of black juice, and said, "You look scared, adept. You should be."

Grey Cloak spun the rod like a windmill. "Scared? I'm only getting warmed up." With his free hand, he grabbed a few coins. "If you ask me, you're the one that looks scared—and ugly. It's an awful combination for the likes of you, Flat Nose."

Commander Slaught charged with a guttural battle roar.

Summoning more wizardry, Grey Cloak filled the coins with energy and flung them into the bearish man's path.

The coins exploded against Commander's Slaught's shield and armor and knocked his feet out from under him. Before he could rise, Grey Cloak stepped on his sword arm and pointed the glowing head of the rod at the man's throat.

"Nice trick, boy," Commander Slaught said with a snarl. "I've never seen that one before. Go ahead. Kill me, then."

"No, I have something else in mind." He poked the rod against Commander Slaught's shoulder. "This is going to hurt."

Commander Slaught gave a crooked grin. "Not as much as you think."

Chills raced down Grey Cloak's spine. He turned his head over his shoulder but not before Fredrake's tail got the best of him. *Whack!*

He tumbled through the air, skipping over the tall grasses. He rose to his elbows. Spots were in his eyes, and every rib throbbed. The first thing he saw was Fredrake coming with a mouthful of flames ready to consume him.

Before the dragon unleashed its fiery breath, Dyphestive clobbered it in the jaw with his rock-hard fist.

The dragon spat orange flames into the air.

He punched it again. *Whop!*

And again. *Slug!*

The dragon staggered away on its four legs and crashed into the grasses.

"What are you doing?" the Risker shouted. His mouth gaped as he glanced between the dragon and Dyphestive. He pulled out his sword. "I've never seen a man knock out a dragon before. Impossible!" He advanced on Dyphestive and brought down a two-handed swing.

Dyphestive rolled away from the blade and scrambled back to his feet. He raised his fists and lowered his shoulders into a boxer's stance.

The Risker looked at him and asked, "Are you a fool? Your fists are no match for my steel! I'll cut off your fists and feed them to my dragon!" He attacked.

Dyphestive knew the Risker wasn't a natural like him. The Risker had to use a dragon charm, which meant he was ordinary. Just how ordinary the man was about to find out. Dyphestive timed the man's strike, caught his sword arm by the wrist, and punched him hard in the armor of his belly.

"Oof!" The Risker fell to his knees and doubled over. His sword fell from his fingertips, and he gasped and wheezed.

Dyphestive grabbed the man's collar and jerked him up. He planted his fingers around the dragon charm embedded in the man's chest plate and ripped it out. It was no larger than a coin in his small hand. "Shiny."

He stuffed it into his pocket and heard Grey Cloak cry, "Dyphestive!"

As Roffik's dragon crushed Anya with its body, she looked the orcen Risker in the eye and said, "Don't worry. You won't see me die today." Her eyes turned into silver flames, and the sky rumbled.

Roffik gave a puzzled expression and looked up.

Anya's lightning came down. White-hot cords of energy lanced Roffik and his dragon. They spasmed all over.

Roffik's teeth clattered. His armor started to smoke from within.

The dragon coiled its tail and rolled over, tossing and turning.

Anya found her Sky Blade and rose to her feet. She calmly strode over to Roffik's trembling form and, with a single swing, took his head from the top of his shoulders. She looked down at his head in the grass. His eyes were still wide open. "I tried to warn you."

Then Grey Cloak cried, "Dyphestive!"

The dark sky turned into daylight when she turned.

Fredrake blasted a mountain of fire out of his great jaws, turning the area into pure flames. Grey Cloak's voice came from inside the dragon fire, and his screams were snuffed out by the sound of its roar.

Chasing Dyphestive, Anya raced toward the grand dragon attacking Grey Cloak. She crossed the distance in a moment and closed in on the dragon with her sword raised high. She was no more than ten steps away when Commander Slaught came out of nowhere and tackled her to the ground.

They went down in a crash of metal armor and twisted limbs. By the time she wormed her way to her back, Commander Slaught was on top of her with his metal fingers crushing her throat.

33

Dyphestive caught the scuffle between Commander Slaught and Anya out of the corner of his eye. Grey Cloak was being consumed by fire. He made a split-second decision and hurled the dragon charm at Commander Slaught's head. It bounced off of Commander Slaught's skull, opening the skin and drawing blood.

Anya punched Commander Slaught in the nose and wiggled away from his grasp. They scrambled to their feet, charged, and collided, their heads pushing together like rams' horns.

With the fire searing Dyphestive's skin, he turned his attention to the flames consuming his brother.

Fredrake's unrelenting fire sucked the oxygen out of the air, leaving Dyphestive breathless. He fought his way closer and started whaling on the monstrous dragon with his ham-sized fists. The dragon didn't budge. He kept hitting. Iron bones hit dragon scale. *Wham! Wham! Wham!*

I need my sword.

Coughing, he staggered back and sucked in more air.

A streak of metal came down from the sky and pinned itself in the ground in front of him. It was the iron sword, the Sword of Chaos. Without a glance at where it had come from, he grabbed it with two hands and rushed Fredrake.

The grand dragon's tail took his legs out from under him and flicked him away like a log. He climbed to his feet. The dragon fire had extinguished, but the ground still burned. Fredrake rose onto his hind legs and roared like a maddened lion.

Streak had fastened himself to Fredrake's back and hung between the wings.

"Get off of me, flea!" Fredrake roared. He rolled his neck from side to side. "Get out of my head!"

Cinder dropped from the sky and landed across from Fredrake. He wasn't alone. Feather and Slicer were with him. The middling pair chased down and attacked the other middling dragons. Cinder attacked Fredrake.

"Bonfire was my mother!" Cinder roared. "You killed her, and now I will kill you!"

"You're welcome to try, Cinder, but you'll be dead the same as her. The same as the others!" Fredrake bull-rushed Cinder with his horns down. They collided head to head and twisted into a knot of scales and talons, tearing each other apart.

Streak squirted away from the fracas, plunged into the burning ground, and started digging for Grey Cloak.

Dyphestive bore down on the battle between Anya and Commander Slaught. He dropped his sword and tackled the man high.

"I have this under control!" Anya said. She locked the man's legs up in her arms. "Help Grey Cloak!"

Dyphestive got Commander Slaught in a headlock. The man was as strong as a wild bull. Dyphestive held on with all of his strength and squeezed.

"You aren't stronger than me, donkey skull!" Commander Slaught said. "I'm one of the strongest Riskers of all!"

Dyphestive locked his arms around the man's bulging neck muscles. Together, he and Anya got the man on the ground. He applied more pressure.

Commander Slaught's eyes bulged in his sockets. He let out a ragged roar. "You can't put me to sleep!" He flexed, and his muscles bulged like burgeoning roots. "I'm too strong for you! I'm too—"

Dyphestive's squeezed until Commander Slaught passed out. Panting, he said, "He's not lying. He might be the strongest Risker of them all."

Anya freed herself from Slaught's legs. She turned her

attention to the two grand dragons destroying the land-scape. Blood, scales, and fire were flying. "Cinder!"

Fredrake had his jaws locked on Cinder's neck. Cinder's talons ripped at Fredrake's chest.

Dyphestive grabbed the Sword of Chaos before Anya could snatch it. He charged at full speed and took a flying leap then sank the blade deep into Fredrake's neck.

Cinder jerked free of Fredrake's maw and shot a blast of flame into the dragon's face.

"Get out of the way!" Anya said as she pulled Dyphestive away from the violent collision of the dragons' bodies. "Cinder is going to finish this!"

Fredrake squirmed under Cinder's fury.

Cinder pinned the enemy under him and wouldn't let go. "Now you will taste the death my mother tasted." Cinder's eyes burned like the sun. He turned loose his flame with a great fiery gust.

Fredrake writhed against the searing heat. The dragon fire turned the dragon's muscle into char, and his majestic body collapsed from within. The geyser of flame cooled, and Cinder walked away from the dead dragon with his horns hanging down.

Anya rushed to his side. Cinder had gaping wounds all over him.

Dyphestive went to fetch the Sword of Chaos. It stuck out of Fredrake's smoking neck. The blade glowed red hot, and the pommel burned to the touch. "Grey Cloak!"

He'd momentarily forgotten about his brother and ran to the spot where Streak, Feather, and Slicer had gathered around a pile of ashes that looked like an extinguished bonfire.

Grey Cloak lay on the top of the pile, covered from head to toe in soot. His eyes were closed, and he didn't appear to be breathing.

Streak nudged him with his nose. "Wake up, boss."

Feather twisted her head from side to side and said, "Shouldn't he be burned all the way to the bone? His entire body is intact."

Slicer nodded. "Good point." He flicked out a single long talon and said, "Let me take a poke at him."

Dyphestive knelt beside his brother and put his hand on his chest. "I can feel his heartbeat."

"And I can feel your heavy hand," Grey Cloak groaned through his cracked lips. "Get it off of me. My ribs are busted, and I can barely breathe. I don't even have the strength to open my eyelids."

"You're alive!" Dyphestive said, elated. "But how?"

"Don't sound so disappointed." Grey Cloak managed to shake the edges of his cloak. "It must be the cloak."

34

A dozen Black Guard riders thundered out of Oldham toward the burning battlefields south of the city.

Grey Cloak flapped the soot off of his cloak and held his aching ribs. "Grab Slaught. We need to get as far away from here as we can." He climbed into Streak's saddle.

"Are we having fun yet?" Streak asked.

"Bushels of it." Grey Cloak grabbed the reins and tightened his legs on the saddle.

The dragon took off at a run, flapped his wings, and rose into the sky.

The small thunder of dragons and their riders left the Black Guard gaping in the midst of the fiery ground. Grey Cloak and his friends flew south until Oldham was far out of sight and landed near the westward hills.

Commander Slaught had woken up and was propped

against a tree with his arms tied behind his back. He spat. "What are you fools going to do with me? Huh?" He spat again. "There will be more Riskers coming after you than flies on dung."

Grey Cloak wandered over to the man and squatted before him, grimacing. "We aren't going to keep your company long. That's for certain." He nodded over his shoulder at Streak, who was baring his teeth. "I'll feed you to my dragon if you don't tell me what I want to know."

Commander Slaught crinkled his flat nose and asked, "And what's that?"

"You were waiting for us outside of the city. Who tipped you off?" He glanced at Anya. Her hair was in tangles, and she had dried blood on her chin. "Was it Atticus?"

"Who?" Commander Slaught asked innocently.

The answer rang with sincerity, but Grey Cloak couldn't be too sure. "Streak, I think we need to apply a little pressure."

"Agreed." Streak put Commander Sloth's thigh inside his jaws.

"Wait, what are you doing?" the commander asked with wide eyes.

"It's called interrogation. Certainly you know all about that." Grey Cloak looked up at Dyphestive, who loomed behind his shoulder. "What do you think? Can Streak's teeth crack open that dragon armor with a little pressure, or will it take a lot?"

"The armor is some of the best. I'd say it would take a lot," Dyphestive replied.

Streak tilted his head in disagreement.

"Listen, striplings, I never treated you awfully in the dragon kennels, did I? I was a fair quartermaster," Commander Slaught pleaded. He looked between the two of them. "I made you two of the best pooper scoopers and kept you out of trouble."

"How'd you catch on to us?" Grey Cloak asked.

"I had a hunch. Come on. I'm an old soldier. When new folks come rolling into town, people are going to talk."

Grey Cloak nodded at Streak. The dragon's teeth popped through the metal and right into flesh.

"Gah!" Commander Slaught hollered. "Come now! Don't make me a cripple. Kill me first!"

Torture wasn't a practice that Grey Cloak approved of, even though the Sky Riders taught it, as did the Riskers. But he needed to know if Atticus had betrayed them, and he needed to know who else might be on to them. And since he'd given Batram the Eye of Enthrallment in exchange for Dyphestive keeping his sword, he had no other way to distinguish the truth from a lie. "I'll tell you what, Slaught. You can keep your leg if you tell me what I need to know. How'd you catch on to us?"

Sweat dripped down Commander Slaught's face in large drops. He couldn't take his eyes off of Streak. "Look, I swear to you, I had a hunch. I swear it. The two of you aren't any secret." He glanced at Anya. "Her either. They've put the word out on you for over a decade. And there are spies everywhere. You can't be stupid. Certainly you know that." He eyed Streak.

The dragon bit deeper.

"Aaah!" Commander Slaught shouted. "Listen to me!" He rocked back and forth. "I'm not a coward. I have nothing to hide. The three of you waltzed right into Oldham, and you were seen. It's as simple as that. People in rotten sludge holes like that have nothing to do but be nosey about whoever comes and goes. They get paid for information." He grimaced and groaned. "You made it simple." He started to laugh. "The truth is, I couldn't believe my eyes when the two of you walked right up to me. A gift."

Grey Cloak stood and pulled Dyphestive and Anya aside. "I believe him. You?"

"I know you can't admit it, Grey Cloak, but I don't think Atticus was behind it," she said with a frown. "I told you I should have gone alone."

"We're in this together," Dyphestive reassured her. "What now?"

Commander Slaught was right. The Riskers would be coming after the battle in Oldham. And they'd left a scent that they couldn't hide. Grey Cloak took a breath and asked Anya, "Do you know another place where we can lie low?"

She shook her head.

"I do," someone with a familiar voice said.

All three of them turned and found themselves facing Dalsay.

"Where in the world did you come from?" Grey Cloak asked.

"The Wizard Watch and High Rock," Dalsay said calmly. "It's been a journey, trying to track you down."

"Maybe if you didn't leave all the time, you wouldn't lose us," Grey Cloak said. "What about the others? Do you know where they are?"

Dalsay turned at the waist and lifted his hand toward the night sky. "They come."

The dragons lying on the ground lifted their heads. Their bright eyes were fixed on the sky.

"Mmm, dinner," Slicer said with a click of his claws.

Out of the darkness, great vultures descended. There were three of them, each with two riders. Gnomes sat in the front of the saddles, and they carried bigger people behind them, who climbed down from the saddles. A few words were exchanged between the gnomes and their riders. Without another word, the gnomes' great birds took flight and vanished into the sky.

The three newcomers walked toward them. Grey Cloak couldn't believe his eyes.

Dyphestive ran right for them and hollered, "Zora!" He picked her up and swung her around as if she were a child. "Grey! It's Zora!"

Talon had reunited.

Grey Cloak was the second person to give Zora a warm hug. "I've missed you," he said.

"You too," she said, patting his back.

They broke apart, and he asked, "Who were your *new* friends?"

"It's a long story, but they're called sky gnomes. They're from the deep south in a place called High Rock." Zora's pretty eyes widened when she saw all of the dragons. "Whoa. It looks like *you've* made some new friends too."

Streak snuck his head over her shoulder and asked, "Do you remember me?"

She patted his head and said, "Of course I do." She turned to look at him and jumped backward. "Streak! Is that you? You're... big."

"I had a growth spurt," Streak said with a toothy smile. "I'm afraid I'm not as cute and cuddly anymore."

Zora petted his jaw and said, "You're still cute and cuddly."

Dyphestive tried to hug Gorva, but she deftly stepped out of his path. He ended up giving her a handshake.

"Who is this beauty?" Razor asked. He was standing beside Feather and looked at all of her gear. "Look at all of this weaponry! It's extraordinary!"

"I'm Feather. It's nice to meet you," the dragon said.

"Oh, you talk. Wonderful." Razor offered his hand. "My name is Reginald, but my friends call me Razor. I'm a blade master."

Feather looked him over and said, "That seems obvious."

"You know, Feather, I think you and I are going to get along fine." Razor held her face in his hands and asked, "Has anyone told you that your pink eyes are marvelous?"

Feather gave a shy giggle.

Dyphestive approached Zora with an eager expression on his face and said, "With all of the excitement, I forgot to ask where Leena is. And where's Jakoby and Crane?"

Zora's face saddened, and her eyes teared up. Even Razor and Gorva dropped their gazes toward the ground. Grey Cloak's chest tightened.

"What's wrong, Zora?" Dyphestive asked. "What happened?"

"They didn't make it," she said with a shaky voice. A lone tear ran down her cheek. "I-I'm sorry."

Dyphestive swallowed and said, "What do you mean, 'they didn't make it'? I don't understand. Where are they?"

Commander Slaught, who was still bound to a nearby tree, laughed and said, "She means they're dead, you dullard."

"No!" Dyphestive shouted. "That can't be! Tell me that isn't so!"

Zora cowered under his heated gaze. "I'm sorry."

Dyphestive balled up his fists. His jaw muscles clenched, and his chest heaved. "Who did this?" he asked in a threatening tone.

Grey Cloak wrapped his cloak over Zora's shoulder. She shook like a leaf. "Dyphestive. Back up. You're scaring her."

Dyphestive's usual unflappable demeanor had turned to anger. "I want to know what happened," he demanded.

Razor stepped in and said, "We had a run-in with a dragon south of Red Bone."

Dyphestive hooked Razor under the armpits and lifted him as if he were a child. "What dragon?"

Gorva put her hand on Dyphestive's arm and, in a soothing voice, said, "Put him down, please. I will explain."

Dyphestive glared at Razor for a moment and dropped him to his feet. He brushed Gorva's arm aside and said, "Tell me everything."

Gorva nodded. "We were traveling south from Red

Bone, distancing ourselves from the Black Guard and hoping to find you. The Black Guard caught wind of us and chased us down in the desert. Among them was a Risker named—"

"Hella," Commander Slaught injected. He spat. "That is one nasty Risker. I wouldn't want to tangle with her myself. It's no wonder your comrades are dead. What I can't figure out is why the rest of you aren't."

Slicer stuck his snout in Commander Slaught's face and asked, "Do you want me to shut him up?" He scraped his claws together. "Permanently?"

"No," Cinder said.

Zora managed to pull away from Grey Cloak, gathered her breath, and said, "They gave their lives so we could live. It was the bravest thing I've ever seen. I'm sorry, Dyphestive. No one hurts more than I do." She stepped closer with open arms.

Dyphestive turned his back, walked away, and vanished into the woods.

Gorva went on to explain everything that had happened between the moment they began battling Hella and her dragon, Warhammer, to the moment when Crane and Vixen rammed them with the Wheels of Fire. She finished the story at the point where the sky gnomes rescued them.

"I feel sick over all of it," Zora added. "If I could go back in time and fight with them, I would. I feel like a coward."

"You did the right thing," Grey Cloak assured her. "Now you can make certain that their sacrifice will mean something."

"I've never seen Dyphestive... angry," she said.

"He'll understand." Grey Cloak decided to change the subject. "How'd you find us?"

Zora opened Crane's satchel and took out the jewel box. "Crane gave this to me. I assume you still have the Medallion of Location?"

He reached into his pocket and removed the medallion. "I'd forgotten I had it."

Dalsay cleared his throat. "We have more pressing matters to attend to." His haunting gaze swept over Commander Slaught. "And we need to discuss them in private."

"Don't worry about me, ghost. I won't say anything." Commander Slaught spat. "Cause I'm too busy enjoying my chaw. Besides, you won't get very far." He spat again. "Because I'm certain that my allies are closer than you think."

"What's that supposed to mean?" Grey Cloak asked.

Tobacco juice ran down Commander Slaught's big chin, and he said, "We made a lot of noise outside of Oldham." He looked up. "And my reinforcements no doubt have your scent, and they will be coming."

"Reinforcements?" Anya asked. "What reinforcements?"

Then came the sound of a distant roar. Far away, dragons flew underneath the clouds and were headed their way.

Commander Slaught huffed a laugh, spat, and said, "Those reinforcements."

CINDER STOOD ABOVE ALL, with his head held high and his gaze fixed on the heavens. "Those are drakes! Dozens of them! They aren't alone either. I see two grands leading them."

"We can handle the drakes," Slicer said with a click of his claws. "They aren't a match for us."

"That's a lot of dragons," Zora said.

"We've handled their kind before." He started grabbing javelins out of Feather's quiver. "No worries."

"Not dozens," Grey Cloak said as he studied the dragons. It appeared that their group hadn't been spotted yet, as he watched the smaller dragons, little bigger than men, dive to the ground and fly back up again. The dragons would find them soon enough. "Dalsay, didn't you say you knew a place to hide?"

"I did, but we won't make it there in time. It's many leagues away, and it would be impossible not to be seen. I hate to say it, but this is a battle where you will have to fight it out."

"We'll handle the grands." Cinder had nasty wounds all over his chest and wings from his battle with Fredrake. Even his strong voice was weary. "Children," he said as the dragons gathered. "Harken to me."

"I have a dragon charm," Zora offered.

With a nod, Grey Cloak said, "I have one too. Still..." Even with the charms, the battle would be fierce, and even if they won, it wasn't likely that they would all survive. The thought of losing anyone else, not to mention young dragons on their first adventure, was unthinkable. "Dalsay, there has to be another way."

The wizard gave him a solemn look. "The only way is to divide your forces and let one of the groups come with me and hide."

"Decisions, decisions," Commander Slaught said. "Most of you will die. Maybe a few will survive, but I have my doubts about that."

Anya climbed onto Cinder's back. "We'll lead them away. That will give everyone a chance."

"That isn't your decision to make, Anya," Grey Cloak said.

"We don't have time to argue. Cinder and I can outrun them. That will give you time to escape."

"Heh-heh-heh, troubles, troubles," Commander Slaught said. "I like."

Grey Cloak had to admit that Anya's plan was a good one, but all of those drakes and two grands would be even more than they could handle. Out of the corner of his eye, he saw his brother walk out of the woods.

Dyphestive fetched his sword, and with his jaw set, he said, "I say we fight."

"What's it going to be, Grey Cloak?" Anya asked.

He weighed his options. Anya could lead the thunder of dragons away. Dalsay could lead them to another hiding spot. Or they could fight. With all eyes on him, he made his decision. "We will—"

A small bright sun ring appeared on the edge of the forest. It sparked in a spiny, fiery circle and started to expand. It created a portal with a new landscape on the other side.

"This way! This way if you want to live!" Atticus called. He stood on the other side of the portal ring, waving his arms in a circular motion. "Hurry! The portal won't remain open long!"

Grey Cloak looked at the skies then at his companions. "I've made my decision. Everyone, man and dragon, through the portal."

They all hesitated.

"What are you waiting for? Go!" he commanded.

The portal reached its full height, standing over twelve feet tall. Then it started to collapse.

"Get in there, Anya and Cinder!" Grey Cloak kicked Cinder in the tail. "Now!"

"Come, children!" Cinder said, leading the way into the portal.

A chorus of shrieks came from the sky. The drakes had spotted them. Their wings pounded the wind, and they raced right toward them.

Gorva stood over Commander Slaught and said, "What about your prisoner?" She had a dagger in her hand. "Should I kill him?"

"No, leave him."

"You'll regret that!" Commander Slaught said with a laugh. "You'll re—"

Whop! Gorva punched him hard in the jaw. "He's annoying," she said and ran through the portal.

"Hurry!" Atticus hollered. "Hurry!"

The portal shrank to half of its full size. Only Dyphestive and Grey Cloak remained outside. Dyphestive faced off with the first wave of drakes as they landed. They were small like men and had scales like snakes, sharp teeth, and no horns, and the tips of their wings had clawed hands.

Grey Cloak pointed at the portal. "Get in there, Dyphestive! Now!"

"I'm not going anywhere."

Grey Cloak shoved him in the chest, but he didn't

budge. "I know you miss her. We all do. But dying is not how you honor her memory. Please, get in the portal!"

Dyphestive's nostrils flared. "No!"

Cinder reached his tail out of the other side of the portal and wrapped it around Dyphestive's waist and jerked him through the ring of fire.

"Nooo!" Dyphestive roared.

Grey Cloak backed toward the ring as the drakes closed in on him in a rush. Two grands landed with two riders sitting tall in the saddle. The riders both had full heads of wavy blond hair and ugly scars on their faces. It was Dirklen and Magnolia. Grey Cloak smirked as he waved goodbye and hopped through the closing ring.

"WAKE HIM UP!" Dirklen said to Magnolia.

Magnolia returned her twin brother's stare. She wore a full suit of black dragon armor, and her sword and dagger were strapped around her waist. It was the same gear that Dirklen wore. "Don't boss me," she said in a calm but direct manner.

He traced the nasty scar on his face, which Black Frost had given him and his sister years ago. It burned. It always burned. "Do you have to take offense at everything I say?"

"I take offense because you're not in charge. We share authority equally." She lifted Commander Slaught's face up by the jaw and gave his chin a shake. Her nose crinkled, and she said, "He reeks."

"Wake him."

Magnolia's bare hand radiated with energy, which

passed through her fingers and into Commander Slaught's face. His face lit up, showing the skull within for a moment.

Commander Slaught's eyelids snapped open. "Uuugh!" He heaved in his bonds and searched his surroundings. "What? What happened?" His face filled with recognition the moment he set his eyes on Dirklen and Magnolia. "Oh, it's you."

"You don't seem very excited to see us, Slaught. Why, you should be thrilled that we came in time to rescue you," Dirklen said.

"Rescue? Hah!" Commander Slaught spat on the ground. "Cut me loose."

Magnolia drew her dagger.

"No, don't cut him loose yet," Dirklen said.

Magnolia stuffed her blade back into the sheath, stood, and said, "Do as you will, Dirklen. Don't ask me anymore."

"Cut me loose, Dirklen," Commander Slaught demanded.

"Patience, Commander. And you should be more mindful of how you address your commanding officer."

"So you've told me a hundred times."

"What happened here?" Dirklen glowered at the man. "How did they escape?"

"You saw it. Some sorcerer helped them. Who, I don't know." Commander Slaught wriggled against his ropes. "Now will you cut me loose? It's an insult that you interrogate me."

Dirklen punched Commander Slaught in the jaw with his steel gauntlet. "It's an insult that you let them capture you!"

"Dirklen, what are you doing?" Magnolia asked, astonished.

He didn't take his eyes off of Commander Slaught as he said, "I'm punishing this fool for failure. That is what."

Commander Slaught spat out a bloody tooth with tobacco juice. As the juice ran down his chin, he leaned forward and grinned. "Cut me loose, and let's settle our differences man to man, boy."

Dirklen punched him again. The blow knocked Commander Slaught's head back into the tree.

"Huh-huh-huh, that orc hit me harder than you."

As Dirklen drew back, Magnolia grabbed his arm. "Will you stop this?"

Dirklen glared up at her. "Black Frost didn't accept our failure. Why should we accept his? Failure is not an option! And this is the second time this fool has let Grey Cloak and Dyphestive slip through his fingers. How do we know that he isn't siding with them?"

"You are a fool!" Commander Slaught strained against his bonds. "How dare you accuse me of treason? I've been serving Black Frost since long before you existed. I was an adept that trained your father! Did you not see that my dragon, Fredrake, is dead? And you dare call me a traitor. I'll kill you!"

"You aren't in any position to kill anyone." Dirklen pushed Commander Slaught's head back into the tree with his finger. "But I am."

"Listen, you wouldn't have even known about them being here if it weren't for me. Blazes, I didn't even know for sure myself until I saw them. But the moment I received word that it might be them in Oldham, I sent word immediately to you. Fortunately, you were close by. Only you weren't close enough." Commander Slaught spat. "And you dare call me a traitor."

Dirklen's face eased. He patted Commander Slaught on his shoulder armor. "Easy, old boy. No need for the heat. The same as you, I have to do my due diligence. You know that Black Frost wouldn't expect anything less. Wouldn't you do the same if you were wearing my boots?"

Commander Slaught managed a shrug. "Possibly."

"Good. Then we share the same scroll." Dirklen offered his sister a charming smile. "Let's move on. Now, Slaught, tell me about the company that they keep. Who were they?"

"I don't know all of the names, but of course I knew Dindae and Festive. It wasn't difficult to figure out who Anya and Cinder were."

"I can't believe she lives. I would have thought her dead long ago," Magnolia stated. "It must have been she that destroyed the Doom Riders."

"Her and Cinder. No matter. Tell me more about the others," Dirklen said.

"There were middling dragons that accompanied Cinder. I believe they are his children. The orc woman was a natural. I could tell. There was a ghost that was a wizard, a half-elf woman, and a warrior that were brought, along with the orc, by the sky gnomes."

"The sky gnomes?" Magnolia asked. "Why would the sky gnomes be a part of this?"

"They aren't worth the worry," Dirklen said. "Tell me, Slaught, where were they going when they teleported away?"

"No idea. A wizard stood on the other side of the threshold, but I'd never seen him before."

Magnolia paced. "There are many rogue wizards on the loose since the underlings took over the towers. I knew those fiends were nothing but trouble." She asked Commander Slaught, "Who where they going to see in Oldham?"

"I didn't sit down and have tea with them, but they did mention a name. Atticus."

"It's not familiar." Dirklen stood. "We need to figure out where they're going." He spun on his heel, and in a whimsical manner, he said, "On a good note, we know they are about and how many of them there are. With Dark Mountain's eyes everywhere, soon we will find them. I guarantee it."

"And I'll help you any way I can," Commander Slaught said. "Loose me now so that I can get started."

Dirklen's jaw tightened. He returned the man's stare with a deep, penetrating gaze. "I fear you won't be going anywhere, Slaught. Waruum!" he hollered.

His grand dragon wandered over to his master. The monstrous dragon had golden eyes, and his dark scales were adorned with gold in tortoiseshell patterns. He stared down at Commander Slaught with his burning eyes and said in an ancient voice, "What is your wish, master?"

Dirklen gave Commander Slaught one final sneer and said, "The penalty for failure is death. Torch him!" He moved away.

Magnolia gasped.

"You coward! You dirty little scum-sucking coward!" Commander Slaught yelled. "I'll see you on the other side of the Flaming Fence. I'll have my revenge. I swear—"

Waruum spewed out a stream of hot flames. Commander Slaught and the tree he was bound to caught fire.

Commander Slaught gave the most awful, anguished scream. It ended as abruptly as it started.

The dragon flame ate away the man's body and turned the tree to ashes. Moments later, next to nothing was left.

"What did you do that for?" Magnolia asked, dismayed.

"You know why. He didn't like us, and I never liked him. Besides, someone needed to feel my wrath. Why not him?"

38

THE WIZARD WATCH

TATIANA STARED into the Time Mural with her mouth half open. The towering archway showed image after image of people, places, and foreign objects unlike anything she'd ever seen. There were magnificent places, uncanny creatures, and different worlds where monsters dwelled.

And I thought Gapoli had it all. I was wrong. A chill went through her.

"Marvelous, isn't it?" Lord Catten asked, standing beside her. The golden-eyed underling hovered off of the ground and wrung his furry gray hands. "So many dimensions to conquer, so little time. But we're only concerned with one."

"This is what Black Frost wants? A portal to more worlds to feed on?" she dared to ask. She'd hardly uttered a word in front of the underlings unless they demanded it. But at the moment, the devious pair appeared content.

"Black Frost has his motivation, and we have ours. That is not your concern. Your concerns are more direct." From his lofty height, Lord Catten gave her a hardened stare. "Look at me."

Tatiana's gaze met his. Tears from the corners of both eyes streamed down her cheeks. Her mind burned like stoked kindling, but she fought not to look away. She shook, held on, and tore away from his eyes. The next thing she knew, she was on her hands and knees, trembling.

Such raw power.

"Brother, what are you doing?" Lord Verbard asked. He stood behind the pedestal of gems that controlled the Time Mural. His silver eyes showed his irritation. "If you turn her gray matter to mush, how will she be of use to us?"

Lord Catten lowered himself to Tatiana's level. He lifted her chin and said, "I need to know that she is strong enough to take the trip. I believe she is ready."

Trip?

Lord Catten locked a bronze metal collar around her neck. It had many precious stones mounted in it, the same as the ones in the archway.

Tatiana found it hard to swallow the lump building in her throat.

"Rise, helper," Lord Catten said as he did so himself. He rested his chin on his knuckles and studied her disheveled form. "There isn't much left of her, but the collar is ample. I believe it will make the return trip, even if she doesn't."

Lord Verbard joined his brother, and while staring at the ornate collar, he said, "Agreed. It is a marvelous creation, if I don't mind saying so myself."

"As always, we have done well," Lord Catten agreed.

With a shaky voice, Tatiana asked, "What are you planning on doing with me?"

The wicked brothers exchanged glances.

Lord Verbard smacked her across the face. "You don't ask. You do!" He floated to the top of the dais and stood behind the pedestal. "Let the experiment begin." His dark countenance became a mask of concentration. "I'm ready to proceed."

"Turn. Face the portal," Lord Catten said as he twisted her around by the shoulders. "You are going to be a pioneer, human. Can you imagine? Traveling from one dimension to another. And if you are fortunate, you might survive."

Tatiana had come to learn the underlings' chittering language over the years. She fully understood what they were trying to achieve. With the fear of the Figurine of Heroes hanging over their heads, they needed another world to which to escape. At the same time, they were preoccupied with their home world, called Bish. They had more than dimension and time on their minds. She sensed a deep hatred. They wanted blood and vengeance.

Lord Catten pushed her closer to the portal. "Brother, focus all of your energy on memories of our home."

The portal came to life with new images of distant places. The sealed chamber glowed like lightning, and every precious stone in the archway caught fire.

A picture formed inside the portal and swept over a dry and dusty land.

Lord Catten let out an elated sigh. When the image touched ground level, he shoved Tatiana through the portal and said, "Return with the sands of Bish."

She stumbled over the sand and fell. Her hands sank deep into the hot sand. The suffocating heat took her breath. She fought to her feet and shielded her eyes from the brightest suns she'd ever seen.

39

ARROWWOOD

THE LAND WAS green and lush, with bountiful vegetation as far as the eye could see. To the west, the Great River that split Arrowwood and the Wilds flowed fast toward the south. It was night, the forest was quiet, and Talon and the dragons stood in the sloping hills, silent.

Talon's faces were grim and showed signs of weariness. All of them had been banged up in one way or another. It appeared that the endless days of fighting one foe after another had caught up with them.

Even the tireless Dyphestive sat on the ground with his shoulders slumped over his knees. His chin was on his fist as he brooded.

"Where are we, Atticus?" Anya asked. "I mean, I recognized Arrowwood's terrain, but how far have you taken us?"

Atticus smiled and flicked his hands. His red-hot

bracers were still cooling. "Not as far as I hoped I could take you. We are south, across from the elven city of Mortus. I'd hoped to land you farther north, but there wasn't enough time, and this is as far as I could make it."

"You did well, and I'm grateful." She looked over the party. "We are all grateful, I believe."

"I am." Grey Cloak offered his hand to Atticus. "I doubted you, wizard, but you pulled us out of a burning barn today."

"Anything for the son of Zanna Paydark." Atticus bowed slightly. "And his friends are my friends."

"How do you—"

"It's a long story that goes back many decades. But I fear there won't be much time to tell it." Atticus closed his eyes and took a deep breath through his nose. "I sense your enemies will be headed to the same destination. Our head start is only marginal."

"He's right," the ghostly form of Dalsay said. "I don't have any doubt that Dirklen and Magnolia will race to the Wizard Watch to warn them of your presence. They fear the Figurine of Heroes more than anything and have taken many precautions to avoid it and even destroy it."

"True, but they don't know that I have it," Grey Cloak said.

"That might be so, but the underlings are no fools. I can assure you that they will suspect you have it. They are paranoid enough to assume the worst," Dalsay replied.

Zora approached Dalsay with hopeful eyes and asked, "And Tatiana. She is well?"

Dalsay put his ghostly hands on Zora's shoulders and offered her a sad look. "She is a survivor, but she has been tasked with much. I fear for her."

"Then we will save her," Zora said. She faced Grey Cloak and Anya. "We have dragons. We must ride to the towers. With the figurine, you can stop them."

Anya raised an eyebrow and said, "You are well meaning, but you are not in charge."

"I beg your pardon?"

Grey Cloak stepped in and said, "What Anya is trying to say is the Wizard Watch is heavily guarded. There are armies, Riskers, and their dragons. Not to mention that we don't have a way to enter, at least not without Tatiana's help."

"Dalsay can get us in," Zora replied.

"I don't have the same power that I used to, but I can help. I can let Tatiana know that we are coming. It won't be a simple matter."

"You'll have to make it simple," Grey Cloak said. "We don't have a choice."

"The enemy will be looking for us as well. We'll have to move with great discretion, and that will slow us down," Anya said. "The elves have eyes everywhere. There is no safe haven in these lands."

"I thought the elves were on the right side of the rivers," Razor stated.

"Not since Queen Esmeralda has taken over. She is in thick with Dark Mountain," Atticus replied. "There are rebels among the elves that don't favor the queen, but I fear it is a scarce few."

"Sometimes a few is all you need," Dyphestive murmured.

"If we're going to stay ahead of Dirklen and Magnolia, we're going to have to ride the sky," Anya said as she started to climb onto Cinder's back. "We can double up on the dragons, but it will slow them."

"We can't take that chance," Grey Cloak said. "If they're going to warn the underlings, we're going to have to race ahead of them. If they aren't ready for our arrival, it will be far easier to oust them. We might only get one chance. This is it."

Zora gave him a disappointed look and said, "What are you suggesting?"

"It sounds to me like he's *thinking of something* again." Anya blew a strand of hair away from her eyes. "Don't do it, Grey Cloak."

"I have to." He eyed the Scarf of Shadows. "Zora, do you trust me?"

"Well, yes." She shrank back a little. "What are you asking me?"

He touched the Scarf of Shadows. "I need to borrow this."

"Seriously?"

"Please."

"What are your plans?" Anya asked.

"The less you know the better," he said as Zora untied the scarf and put it around his neck. "Thank you."

She kissed him on the cheek. "I don't know what you have in mind, but it had better work."

"Anya, you're in charge. Streak!" he said.

"Right here, boss," the dragon said. He gave a snaggle-toothed grin. "I get to fly fast, don't I?"

Anya huffed. "You get sick from dragon flight."

"Ha, that's only what I wanted you to think." He strode to Dyphestive, who managed to rise to his feet. Grey Cloak had never seen his brother so sad before. "Will you be all right?"

Dyphestive nodded. "I'll see you at the tower."

40

BISH

TATIANA TRUDGED down the slope with the heat of the hot suns on her back. Her sandals felt like boiled leather, and the longer she walked, the more her bony legs ached.

Shade. I need shade.

How long she'd walked she didn't know. She headed toward mirage after mirage on the sun-cracked landscape of a barren and hard world. It had trees, but no leaf bloomed on the weathered branches. Small birds with brown feathers and bright-orange bills gathered on the limbs.

She passed cacti, tall and lean, some towering over a dozen feet tall.

Tatiana ran from a scorpion that was the size of a cat and scurried across the land.

Lord Verbard and Lord Catten live here? How?

Tatiana squatted in what looked like a dry riverbed. She scooped up a handful of dirt and filled one of the pockets of her robes. She added a few fragments of wood and crumbs of rock to it. She didn't know why, but it was her nature to be thorough.

Please summon me back.

She lifted her arms to the sky. "*Summon me back!*" she cried. Her mouth was dry, without a drop of spit to swallow. She ran her finger through the collar that connected her to the Time Mural. The hot bronze burned and stuck to the skin of her scrawny neck. "Please summon me back!"

She coughed the sand from her lungs and climbed up the side of the dry riverbed then slowly turned around and tried to figure out her bearings. She'd been walking away from the suns, hoping that a straight direction would lead her to a road of some kind, but she didn't see roads leading anywhere at all. She walked in oblivion.

This must be what life on the other side of the Flaming Fence is like.

At some point, the underling lords had to summon her return, but doubt crept in. *What would happen if the device failed?* Perhaps she would never return home. She would be stranded in another world that she knew nothing about. *Worst of all, what if it's filled with underlings?*

Don't panic. At least the underlings I know are worlds away now.

The heat and blazing terrain didn't make it easy for her

to enjoy her escape from the underlings, but the newfound freedom gave her strength to push onward. Step after step, she marched across the land, trying to focus on what needed to be done.

The underlings wanted to control the portal so that they could return home and travel freely between the two. Black Frost desired the same ability. If he drained one world, he might desire to drain and dominate others. There was a problem, however. The mages in the Wizard Watch had been studying the manipulation of time, space, and other dimensions for their entire existence. They'd learned little and mastered nothing. But Tatiana had learned a few lessons. Between the Time Mural and the Figurine of Heroes, she had come to the conclusion that the portal could open doorways to any place at any period. It could open the past or the present. Grey Cloak and Dyphestive had proved that in their journey that sent them to the past. And if one could travel forward, one could move forward as well.

What if I return to a far-distant future? What if I don't return at all? Dalsay, I need you.

For the first time in her life, she felt completely alone. Dalsay and Gossamer had kept her from losing her sanity while she served the cruel and malicious underlings. Her friends gave her hope and strength. Even the thought of Grey Cloak gave her comfort. If he could make it back from an uncertain fate through space and time, she could as well.

From somewhere far away came what sounded like a wolf baying. The hair on her arms rose. She looked at the horizon in all directions. Far away, in the opposite direction of where she was traveling, was a pack of animals howling at the top of a distant rise.

No.

The wind had been blowing in her face, so she had no doubt the pack of dogs had caught her scent. Those thoughts were confirmed when the dogs dashed down the rise and reappeared again later on the next rise.

Tatiana ran as fast as her spindly legs would carry her. The sand flipped up behind her sandals, slowing her down. She tore off the sandals and ran with them in her hand. The elven blood coursing through her veins took over, and she picked up speed. Her stride lengthened, and before she knew it, she flew across the hot landscape. But a quick glance over her shoulder showed that the wild dogs were gaining. There were at least five that she could see.

I'm going to be eaten alive.

With the hard surface cutting into her soft feet, she ran. At the same time, she focused on drawing her wizardry from the new world. The underlings had a source of mystic power from their home world. She knew that because they'd been able to tap into her world as well. If they tapped into hers, she could summon the power of theirs.

I can feel something.

She stumbled, skinned her knee deep on a jagged hunk of rock, and sprinted on.

The howls of the wild dogs drew closer.

Tatiana looked back and saw the pack of ugly, slavering dogs closing in. Their hides had patches of hair, and they carried hungry looks in their eyes.

With nowhere but open field to run and the suns dipping below the horizon, Tatiana felt the shadows of death close in.

Tatiana's thighs burned. Her breath labored. The fleeting strength in her limbs began to fade, and her surge of energy slowed.

A cluster of rocks piled on the landscape caught her attention. She fled toward them on bleeding feet. She turned toward a cleft in the rock, leaped the last few steps, and squeezed her body into the seam.

Her fingers twitched as she watched in wide-eyed horror as the ravenous hounds closed in. Her last moments of life were about to be spent being clawed apart in a world called Bish. Her jaw tightened at the thought. She reached deep inside herself, found a spark, and summoned her wizardry.

A radiant shield of golden energy sealed her safely inside the rocks.

The ravenous hounds slammed into the shield. They clawed at it, bit, snapped, and howled. Saliva ran down the shimmering field of energy.

The wild dogs' full weight thrust against it. She held the shield with all of her might. Sweat poured down her face. Her brow knitted. She gave all until she had little to nothing left.

The suns set. The darkness came. And the shield began to crack.

41

THE WILD DOGS YELPED. A strip of sprayed blood painted part of Tatiana's mystic sleep.

The dogs broke off their attack and unleashed their ravenous energy elsewhere. They yelped, whined, growled, and snarled. A frenzied battle took place only a few feet away.

Tatiana couldn't see through the blood-smeared shield into the darkness. But her keen eyes made out a large man beating down the dogs with a weapon.

The sound of metal tearing through flesh caught her ears. No other sound was more distinct than the whistle of steel during battle.

Hack! Chop! Rip!

The snarling and desperate barking ended. Death had made its last call.

A big man stepped into full view and stared through the shield and into her eyes. Smoke rolled out of his mouth like a breath of steam. "You can drop the shield, darlin'. The desert hounds are dead, and the one that ain't dead won't be coming back," he said in a strong voice. "Don't worry. I won't hurt you."

Tatiana sagged into the rocks, and her mystic shield dissipated. She trembled from head to toe, and weariness overcame her. She fell forward.

The man caught her by scooping her into his strong arms and cradled her like a child. His chest was warm and the hairs in his beard fuzzy. He puffed on a big cigar.

"Thank you," she said with a shaky voice.

"My pleasure. I caught sight of you running from the dogs. My, you can fly over the sand like a deer. I hoofed it as fast as I could, fearing the worst, but it appears you have the know-how to take care of yourself." He set her down on the ground. "Are you from the City of Three?"

She shook her head. "No," she said with her teeth chattering.

The big man had a full beard of bloodred hair and bushy eyebrows. His build was broad and strong, and he had a frame that could have been chiseled from stone. The sleeves of his green jerkin were rolled up, and he wore the buckskin trousers of a mountain man. He dropped a pack on the ground, opened it, took out a small fur, and covered her shoulders. "This will help while I get the fire started." He handed her a waterskin. "Drink."

Tatiana didn't drink—she guzzled like she hadn't had a drop of water in weeks. To her surprise, the water was cool, and it made her swollen tongue tingle. Her trembling came to an end, the tightness in her chest eased, and she could breathe again.

The man had a small fire made of dry branches and twigs burning in no time. He sat down beside her and wiped down his pair of oversized hatchets with a cloth. "My name is Mood."

"I'm Tatiana."

"A pleasure to meet you, Tatiana." He set his axes aside. "You're very lost, ain't ya?"

"That's an understatement." She took another drink and offered the waterskin to him. "I don't know where to begin."

"It's not my business, but I'm glad to help out. Are you on the run from trouble?" He eyed the bronze collar on her neck. "Perhaps you fled from a caravan of slavers? The Royals' dealings never cease, do they?"

"No, nothing that you speak of—well, I was a slave but not the way you mean. My slavers are... well..." She eyed the star-filled sky. "Not from this world." She pulled her knees to her chest and rested her chin between them. "I wouldn't expect you to understand."

"Pretty lady, I can see by looking at you that you aren't from this world."

"You can?"

"I've roamed this world for centuries, and I've never seen the likes of you. Your ears have tips on them, and no woman has run so fast on the sands before, and few men, either, for that matter. Your skin is tan but not by the sun. You're tall, and your build is slight like an underling."

She popped up. "Did you say underling?"

He blew out a stream of smoke, clawed at the white whiskers thickening in his red beard, and nodded. "But the underlings from this world have been long gone. No need to fear them now." He leaned his head over his shoulder. "That look in your eye, it has my skin itching. I take it you've encountered underlings in your past. They've left scars on many."

Tatiana shook her head. "They're not from my past. They're from my present. They're the ones that sent me here only hours ago."

Mood's cigar fell out of his mouth. "Are you certain?"

She nodded.

"They sent you here from where?"

"My world."

"Smallish men." He lifted his hand above his head. "Yea high, with gray skin and eyes that shine like gemstones?"

"They wear black robes and float instead of walking.

One has eyes as pure as gold, and the other is silver. They call them—"

Mood grabbed his twin hatchets and rose to his feet. His bushy red eyebrows knitted, and he said, "Don't tell me —Lord Verbard and Lord Catten."

She looked at him with awe and asked, "You know them?"

"Aye." He picked up his cigar. "But they've been dead for more than a decade, or so I thought. We must go."

Despite the comfort that the fire brought, her feet were chewed up and scorched by the sun. "I can barely walk."

"I'll bind them with a salve that will heal them, and I'll carry you until they are ready."

Tatiana didn't know Mood, but his demeanor gave her comfort. As much as she preferred to be in charge, she had little issue with giving in to the robust man. She eyed him and asked, "Where are we going?"

"The City of Bone."

42

THE ARROWWOOD SKY

"FASTER, STREAK! FASTER!" Grey Cloak shouted. He pressed his body down along the dragon's neck and back and kept his head out of the winds. "We can't let Dirklen or Magnolia get in front of us."

"Don't worry. They won't," Streak replied. The middling dragon's wings stroked the icy winds high above the clouds, and he cut through the sky like a knife.

The Cloak of Legends rustled all around Grey Cloak. Its fabric kept him warm, and its unique abilities allowed him to breathe easily in the frigid climate high in the sky.

"Excuse me!" someone behind Grey Cloak said.

He twisted his head around. "Dalsay!"

Dalsay's apparition-like body didn't falter against the winds. He sat in the saddle behind Grey Cloak as if he were taking in a warm summer day. "We need to discuss your entry plan to the Wizard Watch."

With the wind tearing through his hair, Grey Cloak said, "Well, I don't have one, exactly. Any suggestions?"

Dalsay nodded. "You can gain entry through the roof. I'll have Tatiana watching for you from there. But getting to the roof won't be easy. The dragons heavily guard the tower from all points of entry."

"I know. I saw!" Grey Cloak wiggled the Scarf of Shadows, which hung around his neck. "I'll be there! You make sure you are there as well!"

Dalsay nodded. "I will." He vanished.

"Eh, that was interesting," Streak stated. He beat his wings in long, broad strokes and gained more speed. "Care to share how we're going to pull this off?"

Grey Cloak crouched behind the dragon and shouted into his ear hole. "They won't be looking for us thousands of feet up. That way, you won't be spotted. Once you're above the Wizard Watch, I'm going to jump."

"The Riskers will see you," Streak said.

"No, I'll have the Scarf of Shadows and turn invisible. The Cloak of Legends will break my fall. I'll slip right between them without being noticed at all."

Streak looked back at him and grinned. "You know, you are one smart cookie."

"What's a cookie?"

"Never mind. I'll tell you later," Streak replied coolly. "If there is a later."

Dalsay reappeared inside the wine cellar of the Wizard Watch. The labyrinth of racks of wine bottles had proven to be the only sanctuary where he and Tatiana could meet. He made his way through the tall aisles that twisted and turned but found no signs of Tatiana. He waited by the steps at the bottom of the entrance, hoping to hear her coming.

The ancient oak door at the top of the steps finally opened hours later. The elven mage Gossamer entered. Once young in appearance, the elf appeared haggard, with circles under his eyes and deep creases in his face. His jet-black hair on one side mingled with snow-white locks on the other, and his black-and-white beard was long and tangled. His black-and-white-checkered robes were frayed at the hems of his sleeves and tattered in some spots above his feet. His tired eyes brightened the moment he saw Dalsay. He hurried down the stairs with concern growing on his face.

"What is it, Gossamer? Where is Tatiana? I don't sense her."

The soft-spoken Gossamer replied, "I fear I have awful news to share."

Dalsay reached out, and his hands passed through the wizard. He wanted to shake the elf and shout, "Tell me!" His feelings burned for Tatiana, and he feared the worst. "What happened? Please, tell me."

"I don't mean to come across alarming. She's not dead, so far as I know, but they sent her into the Time Mural."

"*What?*" Dalsay scratched his brow and began to pace. "How long has she been gone?"

"Only a few hours, I believe. The underlings have the chamber sealed, but they've sent me to fetch them another bottle of port. They labor to bring her back from what I believe is their world." He held up his hand. "Have faith. I must hurry back."

"This is madness," Dalsay said in a defeated tone. "Tatiana does not deserve this fate. It should be me, not her. Listen, Gossamer. Grey Cloak comes. He has the Figurine of Heroes. He can banish these fiends. You have to help him get inside."

Gossamer fetched a bottle of port off of the rack and hurried back to Dalsay. "He really has it?"

Dalsay nodded. "He should arrive not long after dawn. You'll need to grant him entrance from the roof and lead him to the underlings. He can finish this!"

"I'll do all that I can." Gossamer hurried back to the wine rack and grabbed another bottle. "This will keep them distracted a little longer. But I warn you, and I'll warn Grey Cloak. They are ready for him. They have the Wizard

Watch enchanted to protect them. And they hide inside that chamber. Even with the figurine, it will be difficult."

"He knows this, as do I, but I believe this is our only chance to survive. And it might be our only hope to get Tatiana back."

Gossamer gave Dalsay a firm nod and hurried up the stairs. "I will do my part. You stay out of sight." He closed the door behind him, leaving Dalsay alone in the cellar.

Perhaps Gossamer can't enter the chamber, but I can. I need to see what the underlings are doing. I need to save Tatiana. He balled up his fists. *I will save Tatiana, no matter the cost.*

43

ARROWWOOD (THE WILDS)

"BEFORE YOU DEPART, I had something else prepared for you, even though I'm not sure that it still fits into your plans." Atticus put two fingers to his lips and let out a sharp whistle. Three gourn wandered out from the cover of the forest. The towering dragon horses were saddled and equipped with traveling gear. Their orange eyes were simmering flames. "They are yours, assuming you can control them."

Anya climbed down from Cinder's saddle and approached the gourn. "How did you acquire them?"

"We have allies that continue to fight the good fight. I put the word out quickly when you arrived." Atticus rubbed the scales on the neck of one of the gourn. The beast huffed breath like smoke. "Like elven stallions, these creatures enjoy the Wild. It is a sanctuary for them."

Slicer sniffed one of the gourn. "What are we going to do with these? They can't fly."

"Is flying the best option?" Zora asked. "If you take to the air, you might be seen. Perhaps it's better to stay on the ground."

"What do you know about the skies?" Anya interjected. "I'll decide the best course of action. If we act now and fly unencumbered, we might be able to cut off Dirklen and Magnolia. We can stop them before they arrive at the Wizard Watch. It will be a blow to Dark Mountain."

Zora asked, "Do you think that's wise? And what if you fail? We are all dead? We need to approach the Wizard Watch with discretion. Besides, I don't know anything about fighting on dragons."

"I'll teach you," Feather said to Zora. She bumped the elf with her snout. "We'll fly well together. And I like your spirit."

Anya's jaw tightened. "If there is an opportunity, we shall take it. The dragons will fly ahead and prepare an ambush. If you wish to come, you may come. But we will have to leave others behind. We must fly fast."

"Then we will ride the dragons," Zora said.

"We need speed to be successful. The middlings will be slowed with more than one rider. Some of you will have to stay behind," Anya said as she climbed back onto Cinder. "Make your decision quickly."

Zora made a quick count. Excluding Anya and Cinder,

there were four riders and only two more dragons. She assumed that Dyphestive would take one dragon, which meant that she could take another dragon, perhaps Feather. She removed the dragon charm from the satchel. The precious stone twinkled in her palm. She showed it to Feather. "Do I need this?"

Feather studied the stone. "It's very pretty. Is it a gift?"

"No, but I'm not a dragon rider."

"After today, you will be. Get on, little sister. Feather will take care of you."

"That settles it," Anya said. "Zora and Dyphestive will fly with me. What about you, Atticus?"

"My part here is finished," the wizard stated. "I need to be elsewhere. May the Lords of the Air be with you." He walked into the forest and vanished in the leaves.

Gorva approached Zora and asked in a low voice, "Are you certain that you want to do this? I think you should stay with us."

"I need to keep an eye on Anya. I can't explain it, but I feel obligated."

Gorva nodded. "Try not to let her do anything stupid before we arrive at the tower. Though I appreciate her aggression, I fear it is misguided."

Slicer lowered himself in front of Dyphestive and asked, "Are you ready to ride the skies again?"

With a grim expression on his face, Dyphestive

removed his sword and gear from Slicer's saddle and started attaching it to one of the gourn.

"Dyphestive!" Anya said in an alarmed voice. "What are you doing?"

He stuck his big boot into the gourn's stirrup and swung his leg over the saddle. Tucked inside his belt was a dyed-black leather mask like the Doom Riders wore. He slipped it over his large head. The imposing terror Iron Bones was born again.

Zora stepped backward as Dyphestive turned the fire-breathing beast north and rode away.

Razor mounted a gourn and trailed after Dyphestive.

"I'll keep them company," Gorva said to Zora as she filled another gourn's saddle with her big frame. "You go with them. See you at the tower." She dug her heels into the gourn's ribs and traveled into the woodland.

Slicer started clicking his razor-sharp talons together and asked, "Father, can I go with them?"

"No, son. You're staying with us. We'll need all of the dragon power we can muster for the fight ahead," Cinder replied.

"As long as you're promising a fight, I'm ready," Slicer replied.

Feather nudged Zora with her snout. "Put that bauble away and get on."

Zora placed the dragon charm in the satchel and tied

the satchel down. She made herself comfortable on Feather's saddle. "I'm not used to this."

"You flew on those ugly birds, didn't you?" Feather said. Zora nodded.

"Then don't worry. This will be better." Feather spread her wings. "And much, much faster."

Anya and Cinder took the lead and vaulted themselves into the sky. Slicer took off next, leaving Feather and Zora alone in the grove.

Zora could feel great warmth in the saddle caused by Feather's heat. It comforted her.

"Hold tight," Feather said. She flapped her wings, took off running, and launched herself into the air. "Ride the sky!" she shouted.

With exhilaration coursing through her veins, Zora couldn't help but holler back, "Ride the sky!"

44

BISH

A CITY CONCEALED behind a wall made from great stones loomed on the horizon. Its tower walls were made from crude hunks of rock stacked over fifty feet tall. Beyond the walls, the spires of great castles could be seen. Their towers shone with many colors against the suns' bright rays. On those castle turrets were banners that flapped in the hot, stiff winds. The scene took Tatiana's breath away.

"That's the City of Bone or the City of Stone?" Tatiana asked Mood.

"Har-har. The city is founded on the bones of the dead that built it."

"It doesn't have a very inviting appearance, but it's monstrous."

"It's the largest city in all of Bish. The Star City, some

call it." He looked down at her feet. "How are your toes holding up?"

Tatiana had been walking well the last few leagues. Her feet were sore but nothing like before thanks to the blue salve that Mood had wrapped them up with. "Much better. I'm tired, but I can finish the walk."

Far away, a steady stream of traffic followed the main road toward the southern gate of the city. People rode on wagons or walked. Flocks of livestock grazed the land as well. Closer to the gate were clusters of large crowds that had set up camps.

"You'll have to bribe the City Watch to enter," Mood said. He stuffed a small leather purse into her hand. "Offer one gold, but only give them two at most. If they don't yield, come back. I'll be watching for you."

She gave him a surprised look and asked, "You aren't coming?"

Mood rolled his cigar from one side of his mouth to the other. "My kind built this city. But we aren't welcome. It's humans only."

Tatiana studied his broad face. His features were strong and hard, but unlike a man, he appeared more fortified. "What are you?"

"I'm a giant dwarf called a Blood Ranger. But don't fret, lass. I don't have a taste for the city. It's the wilderness for me," he said with a wink. "Can you remove that collar?

Those stones are worth a fortune, and if someone sees it, they won't hesitate to cut your head off to get it."

She touched her collar and said, "No, I have to keep it in place. I can't return home without it."

Mood gently adjusted the cowl he'd made that covered her head from the hot sun. "That ought to do."

She leaned over and kissed his cheek. "Thank you, Mood. I appreciate your kindness."

"Ho-ho!" He rubbed his cheek. "Then I'll remember to stay kind. When you enter the city, give an urchin a couple of coppers from your pouch. Tell 'em to take you to the Drunken Octopus. Tell Sam the barkeep that Mood sent you and you're looking for Venir. He'll set you up."

The name rang familiar. "Venir?"

Mood gave her a quick hug. "Go."

Following Mood's instruction, Tatiana made her way to the city, fought through the desperate crowds at the gate, found a guard, and bribed him. The soldier wore a brown cap with a short black bill, and he had an ugly scar down the middle of his chin.

"Follow me," he said in a gusty voice. He pushed through the knots of people and beat a few of them back with a notched club.

The main portcullis was made of solid steel and straps of iron. Its teeth were set in the stones, and a handful of dead people were crushed in its mighty jaws.

"Some people didn't make it the last time the gate

opened," the soldier said. "But for you, you'll make it fine." He led Tatiana into a stone corridor that was under heavy guard. It was a smaller pedestrian lane that handled a thinner flow of traffic. He pushed open a metal gate at the end of the path, stepped aside, and said, "Welcome to Bone."

She passed through.

The soldier slammed the gate closed and added, "Enjoy yourself."

She absentmindedly rubbed her wrist and had a feeling that she'd just been thrown into prison. "Thank you," she murmured.

A wide road made of well-maintained cobblestones ran from the southern gate all the way to the far side of the city, where the road joined with another. Men and women rode on horses or in carriages, and many travelers were on foot. It didn't take Tatiana long to notice that she wasn't the only one that wasn't human. She'd asked Mood about elves on her journey, but he said he'd never heard of them.

I'd better keep my ears covered.

As she wandered the streets, she felt a little girl tugging on her robes.

"Hello," the little girl said. She was a pitiful-looking child with dirty brown hair hanging over her eyes. The clothes she wore were in ragged condition, and she only had one sandal on her foot. "Can you give me money so I can buy food?"

Tatiana's heart swelled. She knelt, touched the girl's dirty cheek, and said, "I'll be glad to help. But first, can you help me?"

The child eagerly nodded.

"Do you know a place called the Drunken Octopus?"

"Why would you want to go there? It's in the eastern quadrant." The girl shrugged. "But I'll be happy to take you for two coppers."

"I'll give you five if you can get me there quickly," she said.

The child's smile had two front teeth missing. "Done!"

The City of Bone proved to be a massive network of streets and buildings hidden behind its great walls. Every street ran as straight as an arrow, and the alleys were the same.

The little girl held Tatiana's hand the entire time as she pulled her down the roads and alleys at a brisk pace. Every few blocks or so, the little girl would say, "We're almost there."

Finally, they entered a narrow stretch of road in a run-down district where the buildings were in poor condition and the smell of refuse lingered strongly in the air. The last street they took led to a tavern on the edge of an alley. Its walls were bricked and stained with whitewash and mire. A sign hung from two chains, one of which was broken, leaving the sign dangling on one side. The chipped and faded raised lettering was painted bloodred. It read: The Drunken Octopus.

Tatiana filled the little girl's palm with many coins and said, "Thank you."

The little girl jumped with glee, and without a word of thanks, she took off running at full speed and ducked into the next alley.

Tatiana approached the threshold, took a breath, and entered.

45

THE ARROWWOOD SKY

High above the clouds, Streak circled in a slow, lazy pattern. He hung his head and said, "I can see the tower, boss. Are you ready?"

"No," Grey Cloak admitted. "Listen, don't hang around up here. Go back and join the others. Let them know that you dropped me off, so to speak."

"I'll wait until you land."

"You won't be able to see me."

"Oh yeah." Streak nodded. "But be careful around the dragons that are circling. They might not see you, but they can feel and smell."

"Thanks for the warning." Grey Cloak lifted the Scarf of Shadows over his nose and watched his fingers turn invisible. "This is odd. I feel as if I don't exist, even though I know I do." He leaned over and took a long look. He could only make out the rough outline of the green tops of the forested landscape, but there was a distinct circle, a small one at that, far, far below. Even his keen elven sight wasn't nearly as good as a dragon's. "Are you certain that's the tower?"

"Don't you see the dragons flying around it?"

"No." Grey Cloak patted his dragon on the neck. "Remember, go back to the others. I'll be fine. Thanks, Streak."

"Anytime."

Grey Cloak took a deep draw of air through his nostrils and stood on top of the saddle. He turned around and inched his way toward Streak's tail.

"Break a leg!" Streak said.

"Why would you want me to do that?"

"It's only a saying, you see. If I say it, it won't happen."

"Ah, thanks for the words of wisdom. See you soon, I hope." With the Rod of Weapons in one hand, Grey Cloak dove headfirst off of the dragon. His cloak billowed around his body, and slowly, it turned him right-side up. He could see Streak looking down at him. The dragon waved a wing at him and winked.

The freefall moved at a slow pace.

At this rate, I won't land on the tower until tomorrow. I need to go faster.

Grey Cloak wore the cloak like a second skin, and he had some control over its actions. It seemed to work intuitively based on his needs. He gathered the folds of his garment around him, and he began to descend faster. *That's better.*

It wasn't long before he was able to get a closer look at the landscape. He even made out the top of the tower, but it was to the right of his position. *Oh no!*

He spread the edges of his cloak out like wings and started to glide toward the tower until he centered himself back above the spire.

The dragons came into closer view. Some of the middling dragons circled the tower in a wide area, while others crisscrossed right over it.

Zooks. That's going to be a problem. I might land right on top of one.

Grey Cloak slowed his fall and timed their patterns. Four of the twelve middlings he could see crossed over the top of the tower in different stages, but there was a gap in time between them that lasted several seconds. If he timed it right, he shouldn't have any trouble dropping in between them without being noticed.

Those underlings really must be paranoid. Can't say I blame them. After all, I'm coming.

With no more than one thousand feet to go, he envisioned his plan. He would slip between the dragon forces and wait on the top of the tower. Though he would prefer to gain entry at night, the dawn had broken, and he had no choice but to land in broad daylight.

The dragons didn't break their pattern, and their timing couldn't have been more perfect.

Grey Cloak tightened his cloak and began to drop faster.

This is going to work perfectly! I'm good!

He picked up speed. The Scarf of Shadows slipped off of his head. His body instantly reappeared.

Zooks!

Streak's eyes grew wide the moment he saw Grey Cloak appear. His pink tongue flicked out of his mouth. "Don't worry, boss. I'm coming." He lowered his head, folded his wings, dropped like an anchor in the sky, and dove.

46

GREY CLOAK CLAWED at the air. His gaze moved between the dragons below his feet and the Scarf of Shadows drifting above his head.

If one of those dragons sees me, I'm dead.

The Cloak of Legends fluffed out, and his descent began to slow. He stretched toward the scarf, which twirled lazily in the air. He fell slowly, but the scarf didn't drift any faster.

Slower, cloak! Slower!

He looked down. A Risker crossed over the top of the tower.

My timing is way off.

It didn't help that the tower had a flat, round roof of nothing but open space. If he landed, he would have no place to hide.

Using the Rod of Weapons as an extension of his arm, he lifted it toward the scarf while using his free hand to try to swim upward. He kicked like a swimming frog. "Slow down, Cloak. Slow down!"

He caught the scarf on the rod and hooked it.

Sweet apples!

He caught Streak coming his way and gave him a frantic wave. He put the scarf on and watched Streak peel away and fly back into the clouds. Grey Cloak had vanished again, and when he looked down, he was only yards away from a perfectly timed landing on the back of a dragon.

Zooks!

He collapsed the cloak around him and whizzed straight down, slipping right in front of the dragon's nose.

The middling beast reared, bucked, and snorted.

Grey Cloak floated behind its belly and watched the Risker jerk on the reins and holler, "Simmer down!"

One hundred feet later, Grey Cloak made a soft landing on the top of the tower. There wasn't an entrance of any sort. Each and every stone was intricately locked together.

A dragon passed overhead with its eyes gazing downward at the roof. Wings flapping, it flew on by.

Now I'm here. Now I wait.

The roof tiles and stones came to life. They shifted, turned, twisted, and dropped into a spiral staircase leading down into the tower.

Someone called softly, "Hurry, Grey Cloak. Hurry!"

Gossamer's tired appearance took Grey Cloak by surprise. The youthful visage of the black-and-white-clad elf had become shabby, and his limbs were rawboned. "It looks like the years haven't been kind to you, Gossamer."

The wizard squinted. "I hear you, but I don't see you."

"Sorry." He pulled down the scarf and reappeared. "Is that better?"

Gossamer gave an affirmative nod. "You've hardly aged a day at all. A good thing."

"So, where's Tatiana?" he asked as he scanned the room. He was inside a corridor made of the same black stone as on the outside of the tower. Every several feet, a single rock glowed, which cast a soft illumination. "Is she well?"

"I fear not. Come. I'll explain." Gossamer led the way down the corridor, and he walked with a subtle limp. "Tatiana has served the underlings against her will for the past decade. I believe they have sent her through the Time Mural into another world."

"Are you serious?"

Gossamer nodded. "It only happened hours ago. Not long before you came and Dalsay arrived. He is, well, spying, I believe."

"Well, take me to them quickly so that I can put an end to all of this madness I started."

Gossamer stopped and faced him. "It won't be easy. The underlings are well prepared for this day. They have taken precautions that will see to it that you cannot enter their chamber."

"Have you been inside?"

"I have. But not recently."

"Then how do you know Tatiana is gone?" Grey Cloak asked.

"She conferred their plans to me. This day has been coming for a long time, and she has not reported back." Gossamer patted his belly. "My gut instinct tells me that the worst has happened." He passed through a small archway and entered another corridor. "You know the feeling, don't you?"

"I do."

Grey Cloak blindly followed the mage through the twisting corridors and archways on what seemed like a pointless journey. He grabbed Gossamer by the robes and said, "Where are you taking me? This is silly."

"No, no," Gossamer said, shaking his head. "We are avoiding their snares and traps. And only a wizard can walk through these walls without being molested by the guardians inside the towers."

"That's the first I've heard of guardians."

"Believe me. The less you know, the better." With a wave of his hand, a stone wall revealed another archway. "In here, quickly."

They stepped into a secret alcove that was a dead end and contained nothing.

Gossamer held a finger to his lips. He passed his free hand over the wall again. The wall reappeared, sealing them inside, but it was translucent. He nodded forward.

Something crept down the corridor. It came from the direction they were moving. It was a giant snake with pure-white scales and no eyes, and it walked on tiny legs like a centipede. Its body wiggled as it slithered by, its black tongue flicking out of its mouth.

The guardian was one of the ugliest creatures Grey Cloak had ever seen. He'd never even imagined such a creature. It must have crept out of the foulest bowels of the land. Once it passed, another guardian trailed along behind it. It was a skeleton of a man, wearing the robes of a wizard. It passed by as silently as a ghost.

They waited. When the guardians were long gone, Gossamer reopened the secret entrance.

"Those are the guardians?" Grey Cloak asked.

"Some of them. Come this way. We need to double back. There will be more of them."

Gossamer picked up the pace. He entered a man-sized shaft that lowered them down to the other levels. At the bottom, Grey Cloak caught a glimpse of the great fountain he'd seen the last time he was in the tower. It had three tiers, and the vibrant water that had once flowed abundantly had slowed to a trickle.

"Wait here," Gossamer said.

"What? Why? Where are you going?" Grey Cloak asked.

"I need to make assurances that the way is clear. We're close, and you will be safe until I return." Gossamer offered a grim smile. "These chambers don't draw attention or traffic, but stay close to the walls." He walked away at a brisk pace, passed through another archway, and was gone.

Grey Cloak's fingertips tingled. He couldn't shrug off the sense of doom that surrounded him. He waited, with every moment feeling like forever. He could feel his heartbeat in his ears.

Something's wrong.

Two figures slunk out of the archway on the other side. They split up and made their way to the sides of the fountain. They were the guardians.

47

SLICER SAT on a perch in the heights of the towering trees. His dark eyes were fixed on the southern skies. Every so often, he flexed his wings, which were folded down his back. His tail hung down from the massive branch, and it flicked from side to side. Down on the ground, all eyes were on him.

Zora had never stood in a forest that had been so quiet before. The birds were silent, and the breeze had died down to nothing. There was a gnawing in her stomach, too, that wouldn't go away, and she avoided speaking to Anya. She hung close to Feather. The short flight had been spectacular and frightening at the same time.

Nearby, Anya paced with her arms crossed, while one hand picked at her lower lip. Stormy-eyed, she didn't even glance Zora's way.

Cinder was another matter. He sat on his back legs, a picture of calm with eyes full of wisdom.

"This will be my second battle," Feather said quietly. "I hope it isn't my last."

"Don't say that. You're too young to die, aren't you?" Zora replied.

"I'm young but full grown. I'm ready." Feather wiggled her back. "I have plenty of weapons. Don't hesitate to use them. I won't be hesitating to use mine."

"You're too young to be fighting. Aren't you scared?"

Feather shook her head. "Dragons aren't scared of anything."

"Well, I'm scared for you." Zora picked up a stick and chucked it away. "Being scared isn't the worst feeling before battle. It can give you an edge."

Feather winked at her. "If you say so."

Zora had been around for their last encounter with Dirklen and Magnolia in Monarch City. The twin Riskers would have killed them then if not for the Codd's armor and the Figurine of Heroes. They'd had Grey Cloak and Dyphestive and many others too. She didn't see how they would be a match for the pair. But Anya had made it clear that she was counting on the element of surprise. But for some reason, Zora wanted to vomit.

Slicer called down to them by making a strange honk. He waved his tail from side to side.

Anya bristled. She lifted her eyes skyward and spoke

for the first time. "Listen to me. If they are without an escort of drakes, we attack. If not, we'll wait." Her words were directed at Zora. "Satisfied?"

Zora nodded while she absentmindedly wiped her palms on her trousers. She kept her thoughts to herself.

Please don't have an escort. Please don't have an escort.

She'd made her thoughts clear about standing by Grey Cloak's plan more than once. The time for talking was over.

Two grand dragons crossed the sky over them. No drakes were in tow.

Anya signaled Slicer, and he shook his head. "No drakes on the horizon," she said. "Mount up. It's time to attack."

"Wait!" Zora rushed over to Anya. "I've never fought on a dragon before."

"Then you may stay on the ground if you wish," Anya replied coldly.

"I have a better idea," she said.

"I don't want to hear it." Anya started to turn her back.

"You're an idiot!"

Anya twisted around and caught a noseful of the Ring of Mist's spray. She coughed and sputtered. Her eyes turned to flame, and she took a swing at Zora, who jumped out of reach. "Traitor!" She dropped to her knees and pulled her dagger. As her eyelids closed, she said, "I'll kill you."

Zora shrank back from Cinder, who wandered over with fire in his eyes. "I'm sorry," she said. "I had to do it. She might have gotten all of us killed."

"Or we might have killed all of them," he said. "Did you kill her?"

"No. It only makes you sleep. It's temporary."

Slicer honked again. Scores of drakes sped over the treetops.

Once they passed, Slicer dropped down from the trees. "They came out of nowhere."

"What you did took a lot of courage, Zora," Cinder said. "But when she awakens, I have no doubt she is going to kill you."

Twisting the ring on her finger, she said, "But I did the right thing."

"That will be a matter of opinion. For now, I suggest you get as far from her as possible. Feather will escort you south to join with the others. When Anya wakens, I'll try to explain, but I doubt it will help."

Zora departed with her head hanging low. Feather walked beside her.

"I did the right thing, didn't I?"

"That's not for me to say. And we'll never know for sure, will we?"

"But the drakes? You saw them."

"Pfft! We could have handled them." Feather slapped Zora's back with her tail. "Buck up and enjoy these last few hours."

"Why do you say that?'

"Because when Anya wakes up, you're going to wish you'd fought that other battle rather than face her wrath."

"Certainly she'll understand reason, won't she?" Zora asked, but she already knew the answer. And what she thought Feather only confirmed.

"This is war," Feather replied. "There's no room for reason. There's only room for action. That's what Father always says."

"You trust your father completely, don't you?"

"I'll do whatever Father says, because he knows what's best, and he loves me."

48

"I'VE NEVER SEEN the big fella acting like this before," Razor commented.

With her braids bouncing on her shoulders, Gorva nodded. "He hurts. I can see it in his eyes."

"I see more than hurt," Razor added as he bobbed up and down in his gourn's saddle. They were traveling through the thick woodland at a brisk pace. "I see anger. A lot of it. Perhaps you should talk with him."

"Me?" she asked. "Why don't you? You're the one with a persuasive tongue."

"I think your direct speech is more fitting. A few short words of wisdom might send the right message and soothe him."

"You sound scared."

"Me?"

Razor watched Dyphestive riding with a far lead. Dyphestive was a huge man, even while sitting on the back of a gourn. His thick build was a bit of an anomaly compared to ordinary men, even among naturals.

"Well, I'll admit this, gorgeous. I've seen the Doom Riders up close and personal. But none of them put a shiver through me like Dyphestive did when he put that mask on. There is something dark inside of him. It's about to come out."

Gorva's gourn leaped over a thicket of thorns with the grace of a deer. "You should be glad of it."

"Why is that?"

"Because he's on our side."

Razor nodded. His gourn gained speed, and he caught up to Gorva. "He must have really cared about the quiet woman. I never would have figured it. I could see her avenging him but not the other way around."

"Maybe it's not all about her."

"Oh, it's all about her. Haven't you ever been in love before?"

Gorva gave him a funny look. "Don't be foolish."

"What about Crane? Weren't you betrothed?" he asked with a snigger.

"More foolish talk. I admit I was fond of Crane but not in that manner. I'll also tell you this. I'd pick him before I picked you." She sped away and chased Dyphestive.

"You really know how to hurt a fella. Why don't you kick me in the beans next time?" He dug his heels into his gourn and raced after her. "You know what I think? I think you don't want to admit that, deep down, you really like me."

"Is that all you think about? Women?"

"Women and fighting. Or is it fighting and women?" He raised a finger. "Or is it fighting with women? At least in your case."

Gorva ducked under a branch.

Razor smacked into it and was knocked out of his saddle. He lay on his back, groaning. "Love hurts."

Gorva pulled her gourn around. "If you would pay attention to what you're doing instead of talking so much, this wouldn't happen to you."

"I know." He propped himself up on his elbows. "But we've been riding for hours. We need to rest."

"Get up. We can't let Dyphestive get too far ahead."

Razor climbed up to his feet and stretched his back. He rubbed his inner thighs. "I'm starting to chafe."

Gorva rolled her eyes.

"Fine, I'm saddling up."

A woman screamed, then a dragon roared.

Gorva raced her gourn toward the sound. Razor ran on foot.

He arrived moments later and saw Dyphestive sitting in his saddle, staring down at Zora and Feather.

Zora waved. "It's fine. Dyphestive scared the acorns out of me, though."

"What are you doing back here?" Gorva asked.

Zora told them what she'd done to Anya.

"Fiery Red's going to kill you!" Razor burst out laughing.

Without a single word, Dyphestive and his gourn bolted away.

With her gaze following him, Zora said, "He's really upset, isn't he?"

"I wouldn't worry about him. I'd be worried about Anya," Gorva said.

Razor continued to chuckle. "You can say that again."

Gorva glowered at him. "Saddle up. Let's go."

"When I find her, I'm going to chop her into little bits!" Anya swung her sword into a hanging dogwood branch and whacked it off. "Why did you let her go, Cinder? Why?"

"Because I didn't want you to kill her," he said. He clawed at the ground and said, "And she is on our side, you know."

The Ring of Mist had only knocked Anya out for a few minutes, but it might as well have been an eternity to allow Zora to escape. She glared at her dragon. "It sounds to me like you're on her side and not mine!"

"Anya, you know better than that."

"Do I?" she asked.

Slicer was crouched underneath the branches of a walnut tree. "If you want my opinion, she made the right decision. And I wanted to scrap."

"I didn't ask for your opinion either." Anya's jaw tightened. Her fury burned inside of her. She'd been betrayed by a thief, and the thief would have to pay. She wrist-spun her sky blade and stuffed it into her sheath. "You said they went south. Then they'll be coming back north, and we will wait."

With the great trees and their leafy limbs as a backdrop, Cinder lowered his head and replied, "As you wish."

Meanwhile, Anya stormed back and forth until she wore a new path in the grass.

Slicer lifted his long neck. "Someone approaches."

Dyphestive appeared, riding between the trees. He trotted straight toward Anya. His dark mask covered his face, and his heavy stare met hers.

"Where is she?" Anya demanded.

Before she could get out another word, Gorva and Razor arrived. Zora and Feather were hidden behind them.

Anya locked her burning stare on Zora the moment she saw her. "You! You are dead!"

Gorva and Razor, still mounted, blocked Anya's path.

"Get out of the way!"

"Enough bickering!" Dyphestive's voice was dark and

hollow. "Our fight isn't with each other. It's with our enemy, which waits in the north." His gourn moved toward Anya. "If you want to fight, fight them. If you want to kill, kill them. Or you can bicker until your tongue falls out of your mouth. You can kill each other for all I care. But I'm going to the tower, with or without you!" He turned his gourn and rode away. "Eeeyah!"

Anya caught everyone looking at her and said, "Put your eyes back into your skulls." She climbed back on Cinder. "Or do you want the hooded brute to get all of the glory?"

49

As the snakelike guardian slithered his way, Grey Cloak watched the other one in horror. The robed skeleton extended his hands. The bony fingers stretched out into sharp-edged weapons that stuck out almost one foot.

"Lovely," Grey Cloak muttered as he flipped the Rod of Weapons end over end. He summoned his wizard fire, and a charge of energy blossomed on the end of his staff. "Now, which one of you wants to die first?"

The enemy flanked him, hemming him in with his back against the wall. The skeleton glided, and the twenty-foot monster zigzagged right toward him. Its long black tongue began to extend toward him. Sharp fins rose on its back.

Grey Cloak sprang over its head and landed on the other side of its body. He poked it with the end of his rod.

The crawler gave a horrid squeal. It reared on half of

the length of its body and towered above Grey Cloak. Gently swaying in a hypnotic fashion, it flexed and pointed thousands of tiny legs that wiggled and squirmed like worms at him. Hundreds of needles shot out of its body.

Zooks! Grey Cloak shielded himself behind his cloak. The needles stuck all over the fabric. He flapped the folds of his garment and flicked the needles away.

That was close. I need to end this quickly.

The crawler's tongue tried to lasso him. He cut through it with the burning edge of his weapon. The crawler recoiled and scurried away.

From out of the corner of his eye, the skeleton guardian rushed at him at full speed. The sharp, bony fingers slashed at him, as if it were a wild thing from the woodland. Grey Cloak parried its quick hands with the rod and twisted out of its dangerous path.

"You're fast for a dead thing, but I've battled the dead before," he said, referring to his encounter in Thannis. "And I'm more than ready to battle them again." A rush of tiny feet caught his ear. He sprang straight upward, high in the air.

The crawler ran right over the guardian skeleton.

Grey Cloak came downward. Using his rod, he speared the crawler in the base of its skull. He sent a surge of his energy charging into it.

The crawler writhed like a worm baking in the sun. Its foul flesh sizzled.

Poomph! It exploded. Murky guts like mud sprayed all over the chamber.

"Yuck," Grey Cloak muttered as he searched the pile of goo. "And it smells nasty too." He didn't see the skeleton. "Where did you go?"

A bony hand burst out of the crawler's flesh and wrapped around Grey Cloak's ankle. Its grip turned to fire and burned.

"Gaaah!" Grey Cloak furiously jabbed his weapon into the bones beneath him. He gored its shoulder then pierced its skull and pinned its rotting face to the ground. He force-fed it more energy. "Die!"

The skeleton's eyes blazed. The bones in its face cracked. It twitched and crumbled.

Grey Cloak peeled the long, sharp fingers away from his ankle and flung the ancient bones into the fountain. "Nasty thing." He walked with a limp and stole into the nearest corridor. Something was wrong. He could feel the same gnawing in his guts.

Gossamer, what have you done?

He ran and took stairs that wound along the inner walls. Shafts went up and down. The corridors twisted and turned. Every direction he went led him right back to the fountain. Every archway led to nowhere. He was trapped. *Bloody biscuits!*

The inevitable began to sink in. *Gossamer must be in*

league with the underlings. It can only be. Blast his eyes out! The underlings must know I'm here by now.

He passed through another archway and hurried down another long corridor. Gossamer appeared at the other end.

"Grey Cloak, where have you been? I've been searching all over for you," he said.

He caught up with him and asked, "Is that so?"

Gossamer tilted his head and replied, "Are you well? I saw the dead guardians in the fountain chamber. It horrified me. I thought the worst."

"I survived. Now take me to the underlings' chambers, Gossamer, and no more games."

The black-and-white-clad elf paled. "I don't understand. Have I misguided you?"

Grey Cloak shoved the frail man forward. "We'll see soon enough, won't we."

"Er, well, yes. Come, come." Gossamer took off down the corridor with quick but short footsteps. The limp in the leg he'd been favoring was gone. "When I mentioned the tower is rich in deception, I meant it. If we get separated again—"

"We won't."

Gossamer glanced back at him. "Of course." He led Grey Cloak on a trek down unending hallways, archways, and stairs.

Grey Cloak's patience tired. He fed more energy into

the Rod of Weapons and pinned Gossamer against the wall using his forearm against the elf's neck. "Traitor! You think you can deceive me?"

"No, no, I swear it. I am your ally." Gossamer gasped. He pointed a shaking finger at the next tall archway. It was sealed by a solid slab of rock. "That is the chamber. In there. Here I wait." His gaze followed along the ground. "Look, my serving tray." A silver platter had a glass bottle and two pewter goblets centered on it. "They will search. They will summon me. We only need to wait and hide from any guardians."

Grey Cloak lowered his arm. "This had better not be a ruse."

"No, never," Gossamer said. He rubbed his throat. "I want rid of them as much as you do."

Grey Cloak passed his hand over the solid-rock door. It had to weigh several tons. There was barely a seam between it and the archway. He reached into his inner pockets and withdrew the Figurine of Heroes. "Perhaps this is close enough."

50

BISH

TATIANA TRUDGED through thick smoke and made her way to a stool at the bar. The atmosphere in the Drunken Octopus was lively, the language crude, and the foul aroma of sweat and souring wine was enough to knock a stranger over. She covered her nose.

This place is horrid.

The people grumbling at the tables had tired and bloodshot eyes. They played cards and pushed coins that scraped across the tables. Barmaids in skimpy outfits squealed as they squeezed between the sweat-damp bodies, rickety chairs, and tables. They twisted away from meaty fingers trying to pinch their rumps.

This can't be a place where heroes dwell.

"What will it be?" the barkeeper asked. His jet-black hair was thick and short, and his face was pockmarked.

The sleeves of his shirt were rolled up, revealing meaty forearms with tattoos that covered them. His apron was stained and greasy, and he wiped the inside of a wooden tankard with a rag. "Well?"

"Uh, water?"

The rugged-looking man managed a sliver of a smile. "How about a goblet of wine? My finest for a pretty lady."

She nodded. After years of serving the underlings, she hadn't even had a drop for herself.

The barkeep set down a metal goblet, pulled the cork from a bottle, and filled the cup with a purple wine. "Enjoy."

Tatiana fished into her purse, and the man said, "Put that away. The first one is on me. Besides, I don't often get customers with eyes as lovely as yours. If you need anything, holler. They call me Sam."

"Oh, Sam, wait!" She reached over the bar and grabbed his arm. "I'm looking for a man."

He raised an eyebrow. "Is that so?" He put both elbows on the bar and leaned closer to her. "Miss, this is a place where folks keep a low profile. I don't mess in their business. If you try to bribe me, I'll toss you out on your arse."

"No, I wouldn't think such a thing. Mood sent me here and told me to tell you to find Venir."

Sam's eyes twitched. "Stick around. He shouldn't be hard to find." He walked away.

"But how do I know what he looks... oh, never mind."

She took a sip of her wine. Her face soured. "Oh, this is awful. And he said it was his best?"

A patron bumped her hard. Wine sloshed out of her goblet and spilled all over her chest. Without even thinking, she said, "Excuse you!"

"Pardon?" a young woman asked as she planted herself on the stool next to Tatiana's. She was a lioness of a woman with ice-blue eyes. Her golden hair was long and perfectly braided. Strong, angular features without a single wrinkle highlighted her pretty face, but she carried herself like a warrior and wore a sword belt with many blades. Her build was muscular, and her bare arms flexed with every movement. A tight brown vest showed off her womanly figure. She looked down into Tatiana's eyes. "Did you say something?"

"You spilled my wine," Tatiana said as she shrank beneath the woman's intense gaze. She dabbed her chest with a rag. "But I think it tasted better that way."

The woman grabbed her goblet, turned her back to the bar, leaned back as she studied the crowd, and said, "You don't like that wine? Can I have it?"

Tatiana turned in the same direction and said, "You're welcome to it."

Without looking at Tatiana, the woman said, "I heard your conversation with Sam. You're looking for Venir?"

"Eavesdropping is bad manners."

The woman guzzled the wine and wiped her mouth on

her leather bracer. She set the goblet down hard on the bar then thumbed her nose and said, "I'm looking for Venir too. We have business, and I suggest that you don't get in my way."

Tatiana couldn't help but take a closer look at the woman's gear. A short sword was strapped between the woman's shoulders. Her sword belt was a nice rig made from worn leather and had a long sword on one hip and three long daggers on the other. The woman's hands were large, thick, and calloused. It left no doubt that she was good with a blade. Tatiana cleared her throat. "I'm not looking for trouble. I'm looking for help."

"It sounds like trouble to me." She lifted her hand and snapped her fingers.

Sam brought over a tankard of ale with foam that sloshed over the rim. The woman flipped him a silver piece.

Tatiana sat in the awkward silence, observing the patrons. With the woman beside her, she felt like she was being guarded by a hound. Her gaze ran along the rickety tables and disheveled patrons. Candles burned at the centers of the tables in pools of hardened wax. A fire crackled inside a stone fireplace, and a very large, ugly black cat with smoky white eyes nestled on the hearth.

A hardwood staircase with several of the banisters broken or missing led to the rooms above. Men and women came and went, sometimes arm in arm, and sometimes a man had a woman slung over his shoulders. With every step, the boards groaned beneath them.

Tatiana shifted her attention back to the center of the room when a booming voice like a clap of thunder caught her attention. It caught everyone's attention.

"Hoo!"

A huge man stood on the landing at the top of the stairs. His hair was cut to the length of the tip of a fingernail, and a full beard blossomed over his broad chest. He was thicker in sinew than any man she'd ever seen. His muscular arms held up two tankards of ale like trophies. He sucked down one then the other and received a roar of cheers from the charged-up crowd.

He flung his tankards across the room, ripped the railing away from the stairs, and hollered, "Incoming!" He leaped like a great white ape with his arms and legs fully extended.

The patrons gasped. Some scrambled away from their tables.

He did a belly flop smack dab in the middle of a table and crushed it into the ground. Coins and candle flames went flying.

The tavern erupted in angry shouts and jubilant cheers.

The massive man bounced up from the wreckage and shouted again, "Hoo!"

Tatiana glanced at the woman beside her and said, "Please tell me that isn't the man we're looking for."

"Oh, that's him," the young warrior woman said.

"How do you know for sure?"

"Because he's my father."

Is Tatiana stranded in Bish?

Will Grey Cloak's invocation of the Figurine of Heroes work?

Can Talon control Dyphestive before he turns his temper loose?

All of your questions will be answered in Grey Cloak: Book 13!

Don't forget to leave a review for Claws and Steel: Dragon Wars - Book 12. They are a huge help! LINK!

If you want to learn more about Commander Slaught and Fredrake, be sure that you don't miss the prequel to Dragon Wars. HERE IS THE FREE LINK!

Grab your copy of *Grey Cloak – Book 13*, On Sale Now! Click here! See pic below.

And if you haven't already, signup for my newsletter and grab 3 FREE books including the Dragon Wars Prequel.
WWW.DRAGONWARSBOOKS.COM

Teachers and Students, if you would like to order paper-back copies for you library or classroom, email craig@thedarkslayer.com to receive a special discount.

Gear up in this Dragon Wars body armor enchanted with a +2 Coolness factor/+4 at Gaming Conventions. Sizes range from halfling (Small) to Ogre (XXL). LINK . www.society6.com

ABOUT THE AUTHOR

*Check me out on Bookbub and follow: HalloranOn-BookBub

*I'd love it if you would subscribe to my mailing list: www.craighalloran.com

*On Facebook, you can find me at The Darkslayer Report or Craig Halloran.

*Twitter, Twitter, Twitter. I am there, too: www.twitter.com/CraigHalloran

*And of course, you can always email me at craig@thedarkslayer.com

See my book lists below!

OTHER BOOKS

Craig Halloran resides with his family outside his hometown of Charleston, West Virginia. When he isn't entertaining mankind, he is seeking adventure, working out, or watching sports. To learn more about him, go to www.thedarkslayer.com.

Check out all my great stories...

Free Books

The Red Citadel and the Sorcerer's Power

The Darkslayer: Brutal Beginnings

Nath Dragon—Quest for the Thunderstone

The Chronicles of Dragon Series 1 (10-book series)

The Hero, the Sword and the Dragons (Book 1)

Dragon Bones and Tombstones (Book 2)

Terror at the Temple (Book 3)

Clutch of the Cleric (Book 4)

Hunt for the Hero (Book 5)

Siege at the Settlements (Book 6)

Strife in the Sky (Book 7)

Fight and the Fury (Book 8)

War in the Winds (Book 9)

Finale (Book 10)

Boxset 1-5

Boxset 6-10

Collector's Edition 1-10

Tail of the Dragon, The Chronicles of Dragon, Series 2 (10-book series)

Tail of the Dragon #1

Claws of the Dragon #2

Battle of the Dragon #3

Eyes of the Dragon #4

Flight of the Dragon #5

Trial of the Dragon #6

Judgement of the Dragon #7

Wrath of the Dragon #8

Power of the Dragon #9

Hour of the Dragon #10

Boxset 1-5

Boxset 6-10

Collector's Edition 1-10

The Odyssey of Nath Dragon Series (New Series) (Prequel to Chronicles of Dragon)

Exiled

Enslaved

Deadly

Hunted

Strife

The Darkslayer Series 1 (6-book series)

Wrath of the Royals (Book 1)

Blades in the Night (Book 2)

Underling Revenge (Book 3)

Danger and the Druid (Book 4)

Outrage in the Outlands (Book 5)

Chaos at the Castle (Book 6)

Boxset 1-3

Boxset 4-6

Omnibus 1-6

The Darkslayer: Bish and Bone, Series 2 (10-book series)

Bish and Bone (Book 1)

Black Blood (Book 2)

Red Death (Book 3)

Lethal Liaisons (Book 4)

Torment and Terror (Book 5)

Brigands and Badlands (Book 6)

War in the Wasteland (Book 7)

Slaughter in the Streets (Book 8)

Hunt of the Beast (Book 9)

The Battle for Bone (Book 10)

Boxset 1-5

Boxset 6-10

Bish and Bone Omnibus (Books 1-10)

CLASH OF HEROES: Nath Dragon meets The Darkslayer mini series

Book 1

Book 2

Book 3

The Henchmen Chronicles

The King's Henchmen

The King's Assassin

The King's Prisoner

The King's Conjurer

The King's Enemies

The King's Spies

The Gamma Earth Cycle

Escape from the Dominion

Flight from the Dominion

Prison of the Dominion

The Supernatural Bounty Hunter Files (10-book series)

Smoke Rising: Book 1

I Smell Smoke: Book 2

Where There's Smoke: Book 3

Smoke on the Water: Book 4

Smoke and Mirrors: Book 5

Up in Smoke: Book 6

Smoke Signals: Book 7

Holy Smoke: Book 8

Smoke Happens: Book 9

Smoke Out: Book 10

Boxset 1-5

Boxset 6-10

Collector's Edition 1-10

Zombie Impact Series

Zombie Day Care: Book 1

Zombie Rehab: Book 2

Zombie Warfare: Book 3

Boxset: Books 1-3

OTHER WORKS & NOVELLAS

The Red Citadel and the Sorcerer's Power